Rick's Adventures in Paris
Eric Nelson

with illustrations by Riki Kölbl Nelson

Enjoy!

Eric & Riki

Copyright 2022 by Eric Nelson.
Published by By All Means Graphics
17 Bridge Square
Northfield, MN 55057
All rights reserved.
Published in the United States of America.
ISBN 978-1-7367891-4-8

Dedicated with thanks to my wife Riki
for her delightful illustrations,
to our son Benno and our granddaughter Else
for their important revisions throughout the text.

CHAPTER 1

I'm a genius. I wasn't always a genius, of course. I started out as a child prodigy, which, I have to say, is a very strange experience – even weirder than being a genius.

You probably think I'm bragging and that I'm not really a genius, but I'm not and I am. A lot of people secretly hope they turn out to be a genius but they have too small a notion of what a genius is. They think a genius composes music or plays chess or designs fantastic science projects, all of which is true, but that doesn't begin to exhaust the list of genius possibilities. So if you aren't Mozart or Bobby Fisher you think, gee, maybe I'm not a genius after all. Wrong.

You can be a genius at anything. It's not *what* you do but *how* you do it. I'm a genius at making peanut butter sandwiches. That's right, I'm *that* genius. Unless you've been living on another planet you know that I make peanut butter sandwiches like nobody else. I have made sandwiches for rock stars and movie stars.

That's just the beginning. What I'm going to do here is tell the whole story: the behind-the-scenes stuff at "Rick's Cafe", my rock club in Paris; the political controversy that erupted when my sandwiches appeared on the menu of a three-star restaurant; my fifteen minutes of fame on French television and the riot that followed. Danielle would say it's the classic story of love and politics. And it all started with a peanut butter sandwich.

When you are a genius, you aren't discovered so much as diagnosed as having an exotic disease. It isn't infectious so people aren't afraid to touch you. Just the opposite. Everybody crowds into your small hospital room to watch the symptoms of this rare illness. They bring flowers and gifts; they say they wish you well and I guess they do, but let's be honest, they come because they are curious. They stare at you and you know they are thinking, it could happen to me. And they're right, it could. Maybe it has. You can be a genius for years and not know it, carrying the virus around like a secret, a secret even from you. You shrug off the symptoms until one day you go in for a routine check-up and the doctor looks at the test results and gives you a serious, pitying look and begins, "I don't want to alarm you but...."

From that moment on, in the eyes others, you become your affliction. When they look at you they see "genius" and you can kiss a normal life good-bye, which is kind of crazy because what could be more normal than genius? In my own case it was peanut butter sandwiches. Millions of mothers make them every day. Even a rocket scientist could do it. No big deal. Then out of the blue, the doctor sits down at his desk across from you, opens a manila folder and looks at you as if you were already dead. He says gently, "We've been examining your peanut butter sandwiches and we've noticed something that appears to be out of the ordinary." For you, peanut butter has suddenly become a big deal.

Take Mozart. He liked to play music, the kind of music they played back before there was any sound technology to speak of. No radio, no CDs, Internet or iPods. If you were rich you could hire your own house band, but if you weren't the only way you could hear music was to play it yourself. Making music was something ordinary people did all the time, like making peanut butter sandwiches. Or take Bobby Fisher. In the sixties, before there were personal computers, everybody played board games – Parcheesi, Monopoly, Clue, chess, checkers, whatever. Some people won more than others, some were competitive in a fairly compulsive way. So why throw huge spotlight on one kid just because he always puts a hotel on Boardwalk? Why put him on the cover of *Life*? This is mysterious. Once you're diagnosed with genius, people stop acting normal in your presence. No matter what you do, you make others self-conscious.

The thing about my peanut butter sandwiches, they were impossible to explain. How could two slices of Wonder bread with a layer of Jiff or Skippy (smooth or crunchy) and jelly (any brand, preferably the cheapest) be better than Beef Wellington, better than a Big Mac, better than a pint of Ben and Jerry's Rocky Road? What was my secret? I hadn't a clue. If you can't explain something you can at least give it a name and I suppose genius is as good a name as any. Like Harvey the invisible rabbit. Why call him Harvey? Well, you have to call him something. Being a genius is a lot like being an invisible rabbit. People are amazed because they don't see how you do what you do. They don't even see you.

And because they don't see you, they have to imagine you. Mozart stories begin to circulate. You know, those stories about how Mozart invented music two months before his mother went into labor and how he composed "The Magic Flute" in his crib and how he wrote Beethoven's ninth symphony in the back of his spelling book when he was six. Those stories went around about me. When I was just an infant sitting in the grocery cart on my first trip to the store I reached out in aisle 6 and grabbed a small jar of Skippy from the shelf. And later did the same thing with a loaf of Wonder bread. Did this really happen? I don't know. Who remembers what they did when they were two years old? My Aunt Polly Esther swears the story is true but it may just be something she heard and gradually came to believe.

She also claims she walked into the kitchen one rainy morning – I was five at the time –and she found me sitting at a table surrounded by high, perfectly formed stacks of peanut butter and jelly sandwiches. She took one, ate a bite, and had to sit down. It was a while before she took another. Eventually she worked her way, slowly, through the sandwich. The experience left her nonplussed. That was the word she always used in telling this story, which she did many, many times. I looked the word up once: "nonplus'[L = no more] 1. a state of extreme perplexity." Aunt Polly Esther had never been in a state of

extreme perplexity before and it alarmed her. Was she experiencing a "neurological event," something that might require immediate medical attention? Whatever it was, some sort of reality test was called for. She bundled me up and we went around the neighborhood knocking on doors and distributing sandwiches. We returned home and waited and sure enough the calls came – expressions of gratitude, requests for more. Aunt Polly Esther relaxed. She wasn't going crazy.

Aunt Polly Esther has a bed-and-breakfast place though it's not a typical operation. It's in a huge mansion. Three full-time gardeners maintain the grounds and a household staff of three housekeepers. Sounds a bit posh? Couldn't be further from the case. Alice Freelander, author of the most widely read bed-and-breakfast guide in the country, described it best:

I must say something about Polly Esther Potter's oddly named Mildew Manor on Chicago's North Shore Drive. A sixteen-room mansion in faux-Victorian style, the establishment is at once impressive and homey. The high-ceilinged bedrooms are commodious and, when the drapes are drawn, full of light. The appointments in each room range from the gracious to the eccentric: here an exquisite flower arrangement, there a stuffed squirrel baring its teeth.

The house rules, posted in each room, are also, depending on one's mood, amusing or outrageous. Guests must make their beds by 10:00 a.m. and must pick up and fold all personal garments before leaving their room. Then there is "breakfast." Ms. Potter prepares the menu herself: Wheaties in lukewarm skim milk, two overcooked eggs, two very crisp pieces of bacon, two slices of very crisp toast, cold butter, Hills Brothers coffee. Bring your own Alka Selzer.

Why would anyone pay money to come to such a place, even at the very reasonable rates charged by Ms. Potter? Hard to explain. If you like it you like it, if you don't you don't. When I was little I would occasionally stay with my maternal grandmother, a wise dotty old dear who loved me as no one else has and whom I loved. Ms. Potter (she insists on being called Polly Esther) gave me just this feeling. Professionally, I cannot recommend the place. Personally, I adored it. There is, I should add, no Mildew at Mildew Manor. The place is spotless.

If you go, by all means drop by the kitchen during the noon hour. If you do you will be invited to lunch, gratis. This consists of peanut butter sandwiches, sandwiches such as you have never tasted before and never will again. Out-of-this-world, remember-them-all-your-life sandwiches. Delicious is too weak a word. They are not made by Polly Esther but by her young nephew.

Alice Freelander almost got it – the secret of Aunt Polly Esther's genius. Because she was a genius, the best kind of genius, the kind that is not recognized as such. Aunt Polly Esther's genius was to be herself. She was totally and purely herself and in her company you could be yourself too, whatever that was. How did it happen? I don't know. That's the mystery. Aunt Polly Esther had it and Ms. Freelander picked up on it, as did all the other people who were intrigued by her description and came to Mildew Manor. They had difficulty putting it into words. Like Ms. Freelander they talked about grandmothers or tree houses or something like that. They didn't mind making their beds and picking up their clothes. They would linger over the breakfast table and start to confide. "I've never told anyone this before," they would begin. They acted as if we were long lost friends. After they left they continued to send us post cards, Christmas cards, graduation announcements. They became distant relatives.

That's all very nice, you may be saying to yourself, but this doesn't sound like a money-making business. How does she pay her sizable staff and the taxes on a North Shore mansion, much less turn a profit, on the income from this quixotic operation? The short answer: she doesn't. Aunt Polly Esther's bed-and-breakfast is open only during the summer. The rest of her time is devoted to her real career, writing. She is the most successful writer in America today. More successful than Danielle Steele or John Grisham or Stephan King. Like them she is a writer of fiction, though it took her a while to find her form. She tried serious realism, she tried escapist fantasy. She tried satire. She tried historical romance, Gothic romance, teen romance. She tried science fiction and legal fiction. She tried ghost writing memoirs and memoirs of ghosts. She tried detective stories, thrillers, spy novels. She tried children's books and books for young adults. She tried writing about baseball, marriage, and spiritual journeys.

She went through just about every genre known to humankind until she finally discovered the diet book. Her fantasy took flight. She imagined ten-day diets, ten-week diets, ten-month diets. Fruit diets and bread diets, chocolate and yogurt diets, dandelion and rose petal diets, on and on. All of them best sellers. Of course she didn't publish these diet books under her real name. You might buy fifteen detective novels by the same author but you certainly wouldn't buy fifteen diet books written by the same person. Aunt Polly Esther wrote under many pseudonyms. A couple of years ago the *Wall Street Journal* revealed that 90% of the successful diet books in the US during the preceding decade were all written by the same person, Polly Esther Potter. The royalties made her a millionaire many times over. Fortunately not many dieters read the *Wall Street Journal* and her fans (who don't even know they are her fans) continue to buy her books. And she continues to crank them out at a rate of two a year.

"Whether or not my diets are realistic is completely beside the point," she told the reporter for the *Wall Street Journal*. "Even to ask the question is to show you have no inkling what a diet is. A diet, like the American Dream, is an inexhaustible fantasy. We are a nation of dreamers and so, inevitably, a nation of dieters."

Aunt Polly Esther's own inexhaustible fantasy was Mildew Manor, her dream family, though she refused to admit that to herself or to anyone else. She abhorred the idea of marriage, she said. "Men can't abide a truly independent woman," she remarked once, "as a wife." That was one of her words, abide. "Families are a wonderful institution, I've no doubt," she used to say, "but I can't abide them." This always puzzled me because it seemed that she treated her gardeners and housekeepers and their families as if they were *her* family. They all lived at Mildew Manor and the staff kids had the run of the place. I grew up thinking we were all somehow related, cousins or something. I asked her once why she couldn't abide families.

She mused for a while, then said, "I don't rightly know. The promise to love, honor, and obey a husband just gives me woolen underwear bejeebees. And the thought of all those children underfoot."

"But Aunt Polly," I protested, "I was a child."

She looked at me, shocked. "Good lord, Rick," she exclaimed. "Whatever put that idea into your head?

CHAPTER 2

After Ms. Freelander's description of Mildew Manor appeared, we began to attract more and more visitors, not as a bed-and-breakfast place but as a peanut-butter-and-jelly-sandwich place. Nobody ever showed up for breakfast, everyone was there for lunch. At some point journalists started to appear, people who wrote articles for travel sections of their local newspapers. A couple of foodie bloggers came. Then a guy named Calvin Trillin wrote a long story for *The New Yorker* magazine titled "The Mozart of Peanut Butter" and that was when my hope for a normal life ended.

My parents became aware of what my mother referred to as "this silliness." They didn't actually see or read any of the news stories. They were too busy. And they had other plans for me. My father, who is an astrophysicist, wanted me to become a scientific genius, and my mother, who plays first cello in the Chicago Symphony, wanted me to be a musical genius. They argued about this until my mother read in a psychology book that mathematicians also frequently have an aptitude for music. She shared this information with my father with joy and excitement: in their disputes about my gifts they had failed to recognize the full scope of my genius. I was destined to be both Einstein *and* Mozart.

That I was having trouble mastering elementary algebra or that I couldn't stay in key singing even the simplest tunes did not appear to matter to them. Einstein didn't speak until he was three. Early incompetence, according to my mother, is the surest sign of genius. She often consulted works of psychology regarding my nature and nurture; me she did not consult.

I had this strange feeling my parents did not see me. They imagined me, but they did not see me. This was understandable. My dad, as I said, is an astrophysicist, which means he spends his working

life – in other words, his life – staring into deep space trying to get a fix on something called "dark matter". As a result he has developed a severe case of far-sightedness. He has acute vision when it comes to events that are light-years away but events that are under his nose (his son, for example) are a total blur. When he looks at me I get this eerie feeling that he isn't looking at me but at the quarks inside the atoms inside my head. Once in science class the teacher told us that at the atomic level each of us consists mostly of empty space. That statement shocked my classmates. It made perfect sense to me.

Then there is my mother. As a cellist she is very good at focusing on what is right under her nose. Most of the time it is a musical score. My mom doesn't see me as a collection of atoms but as notes that she must turn into music. When the performance is over she stands up to accept the applause. I get an honorable mention in the program notes.

My real parental unit was always Aunt Polly Esther, because my folks' demanding jobs kept them away from home most of the time. Aunt Polly Esther was mom's older sister. She was fifteen years older and could almost have been my mom's aunt. It's hard to imagine them growing up in the same family. Mom is a fairly intense person. She's very beautiful and is always elegantly dressed in stylish clothes made of natural fibers. Even when she is in a hurry, which is pretty much all the time, every hair is in place. Aunt Polly Esther's wardrobe is entirely wash-and-wear. She is to elegant what dark matter is to matter. The Mildew Manor family was my real family. My favorite "cousin" was Sally, the daughter of one of the housekeepers and a gardener. We went everywhere and did everything together. When I would get fed up with being invisible at home I could rant and rave to Sal; she was a terrific listener. We could have been brother and sister, except brothers and sisters fight all the time.

And then there was Sagittarius. Sagittarius was in his twenties; his parents had been hippies, the kind who would name a child Sagittarius. He was tall and very good looking, had a mustache and wore his hair in a ponytail. We called him Sage (as in Saj). If you spend a lot of time with someone, do you really want to wrap your tongue around five syllables, especially if they're silly syllables? Apparently his folks were really bright people who had read everything and knew a lot but didn't want to be a part of "the system," as they called it. They were long-haired dropouts who formed their own counterculture community based on the principles of love and freedom. Eventually this community consisted only of Sage, his parents and his two sisters. Sage claimed everyone else left because his folks had a very unhippie attitude toward drugs: zero tolerance. They spent most of their time raising vegetables and teaching their kids. They sound like the opposite of my mom and dad except that Sage's father had also been a physicist and his mother played the flute, though she had never been a professional musician. It was just part of her spiritual life. They taught Sage an amazing amount of stuff – he seemed to know pretty much everything – but they never taught him how to fit into "the system." And this was the source of all his problems.

He went to college and although he took a casual attitude toward class attendance and deadlines he graduated with decent grades because he loved to read and write and his folks had taught him how to think in all kinds of interesting ways. He dropped out for a while and went to Europe but he wound up with a college degree. Not that it did him much good.

He wanted to teach but he got fired from one job after another; he had no grasp of how a normal teacher teaches. His idea of teaching social studies, for example, was to break his class into groups and assign each one to write a chapter for a book titled *Sherlock Holmes Abroad*. Each group was given a different country and had to do research to create the setting and characters and figure out an ingenious crime, clues, suspects, and a solution, all of which had to reflect the culture in some way. At the end of the semester each group performed their "mystery" for the whole class and talked about what they had learned writing it. Then all the stories were printed in a book that the kids could take home. They also sold copies, and that's what caused trouble. Some of the crimes were a bit ghoulish – in one the group had a mean mother and father murdered in bizarre way – and this upset some people in the community. For these people there was a difference between normal creative and abnormal creative. This is a problem that goes back to Socrates, Sage told us, who was convicted of corrupting his students with radical ideas. The Athenians made him drink hemlock. I got off easy, Sage said; they just fired me.

His name sure didn't help: Sagittarius Millennium Faulkner. A lot of the time it kept him from getting a job in the first place. As soon as a school superintendent looked at his application and saw that name his fate was sealed. But sometimes the school might be desperate to fill a position a month before the start of the school year. They would interview him and Sage always impressed people in interviews. "I do great interviews," he said. And he did.

It was his interview with Aunt Polly Esther that got him into the Mildew Manor family. She read in the papers a story about how he had appeared at a school board hearing dressed in a clown suit to defend his teaching philosophy. That's just the sort of unconventional behavior that would intrigue her so she contacted the school board, got in touch with Sage and said she would like to interview him for a possible teaching position, as a private tutor. Unemployed, with no promising letters of reference, he agreed to come. That's when Aunt Polly Esther brought us on board and explained the situation. She had noticed that I was not the most disciplined of students. She blamed herself, she said, because she was certain that the publicity and attention surrounding my peanut butter sandwiches were the source of the problem. Something was needed to counteract the

distractions of my "fame," something equally powerful. "I may have found the young man for the job," she said to Sal and me. "I've arranged an interview and I want you to sit in and offer your assessment of his suitability." She was including Sal to get a second opinion. This was a shrewd move on her part. If I agreed to hire this guy – and I could tell she thought I would agree – then I would have at least a modest investment in his success.

So he came and introduced himself. His name, of course, required an explanation of sorts and the explanation led to an explanation of his parents. Aunt Polly Esther was, as I indicated earlier, skeptical of the institution of marriage but the marriage that Sage described could hardly be called an institution and Aunt Polly Esther nodded approvingly at Sage's characterization of his folk's open-ended commitment, and their educational philosophy. When Sage asked if she would like some background on his own pedagogy, she said, "That won't be necessary. I've done due diligence. To my mind the key to effective teaching is asking challenging questions, questions that engage the mind but do not permit of easy answers. So Mr. Faulkner, what is the most challenging question you can conceive?"

"The most challenging question for a child?" Sage asked.

"I do not accept that children are different from adults in this regard. And your potential students," she nodded toward us, "are not children."

Sage thought for a long moment, then said, "My question is this: What question must you ask after you have asked every other question in the universe?"

Aunt Polly Esther frowned and said, "*Must* ask?"

"Yes. It's a simple question but it is necessary because it may open the door to another universe with other questions."

Wow. Just like that he had turned the tables on us. Aunt Polly Esther had challenged him to come up with his most difficult question and – boom! – he had challenged us to conceive of a question, the last question of all questions, and said that it *had* to be asked. He had put *us* on the spot. It was like we were in a game show where he was the Game Master. This was the final episode. Win all, lose all. The grand prize: another universe. The clock was ticking...tick-tock, tick-tock.

"I can't imagine," Aunt Polly Esther finally conceded. She turned to us and we shook our heads. We looked to Sage and waited.

"Have I missed anything?" he said.

We sat stunned. Have I missed anything? How could that open the door to another universe? It didn't sound like a trick, but it also wasn't a very deep question. I knew I would be going over this for some time.

Aunt Polly Esther looked to us and we nodded. "Mr. Faulkner," she said, "the job is yours if you want it."

Aunt Polly Esther did not seek my parents' approval for this arrangement, but she did feel that they ought to meet him. I'm not sure what she would have done if either one or both hadn't approved of him but that didn't turn out to be a problem. When she knew my mother was going to be at home she sent us over. Make it a very casual meeting, she said to me, otherwise my sister may get her back up. So I took Sage over to our place. We were in the living room and I was showing him this glass case that contains my mother's collection of antique instruments, her most prized possessions. As we were peering in I became aware that mom was standing behind us. Maybe she was afraid we would attempt to open the case and take something out, the last thing I would ever dream of doing. I turned and awkwardly introduced Sage, without saying why he was with me. Sage said to her, "Would you allow me to hold that contralto viola for just a moment?" My mother hesitated, frowning. She was not happy, I could tell, about this audacious request from someone she did not know. She weighed her options, then went to the side table, opened a drawer, took out a key, and returned. She opened the case and handed the viola to Sage, at the same time giving me a look of stern disapproval: why had I put her in this position?

Sage took the instrument from her and ran his fingers over it. He said, "Guarneri," then, "The bridge and sound post have been replaced...a beautiful job." He handed the viola back to mom. "Thank you."

My mother put it back in its place and locked the case. "Would you like some coffee?" she offered. "Some poppy-seed cake?" She was smiling as if she had all the time in the world to get to know this fascinating young man.

When Sage met my father the same sort of thing happened. Sage and I were in the kitchen and he was teaching me some chess moves when dad came in for a Coke. I introduced them and dad grunted and told us to continue our game. Sage shifted his Queen.

"Good move," my father said.

"I learned that from a guy from Stanford," Sage said, still looking at the board and waiting for my next move. "He was in physics too. Maybe you know him. Phil Ochs."

There was a pause. Phil Ochs is my father's biggest rival. They are both working on dark matter, hoping for a breakthrough that will win a Nobel Prize. They would not be happy sharing the prize.

"Yes, I know him," my father said.

"This was at a chess tournament in Aspen," Sage went on. "We talked over lunch and he tried to explain dark matter to me. I told him it sounded like the Taoist concept of emptiness. He was quite interested."

"What is the Taoist concept of emptiness?" my dad asked.

"It's paradoxical," Sage said. "An emptiness that is full because it is empty. It's not something I can explain off the top of my head. I'm not sure it *can* be explained. Anyway Phil Och was quite interested so I told him to check out the *Tao te Ching*. Taoism plays with paradoxes very similar to those in physics. 'The best closure has no bolts, yet it cannot be opened. The best knot has no cord, yet it cannot be untied.'"

Dad left and returned with a pencil and a pad of paper. "What was the title of that book again?" Sage spelled it for him, smiled at me over the chessboard and winked. Both of my parents, needless to say, had no objection to Sage tutoring me. They saw him as just the sort of mentor a future genius ought to have. Little did they know.

CHAPTER 3

Aunt Polly Esther now imposed a new educational regimen. There was no point in hiring Sage as a tutor if he had to fight to keep my attention. We were getting requests to do catering: weddings, corporate banquets, birthday parties, political fundraisers. No, no, no was Aunt Polly Esther's reply to all of them. She made no exceptions. Except once.

She got a phone call from the executive secretary of T. Ainsworth Fogdingle, the sixth richest man in America. He was old and had a rare heart ailment, this secretary explained. He had read reports of my peanut butter sandwiches and they had brought back memories of his childhood on a South Dakota farm during the Depression. Death was not far off. He would be deeply grateful if I would consent to come to his place on Fogdingle Peak and make him a lunch of one of my sandwiches. Of course my expenses would be paid and Mr. Fogdingle's gratitude would be expressed in a tangible form I thought suitable.

Aunt Polly Esther could not immediately say no to this request. It wasn't a question of money; it was the sentimental value of the meal to an elderly gentleman living on borrowed time. It amounted to a dying man's last request. The fact that he was rich did not make him any less touching in Aunt Polly Esther's eyes. He had, after all, been formed by a childhood in the dust bowl.

"I want to go," I told her.

So I did. Sage and Sal came along. We would have been happy to take a plane to Casper and rent a car but Mr. Fogdingle insisted that we fly directly to the foot of his mountain in his Lear jet. We landed on his airfield and were escorted to a van. The driver may have introduced himself, I'm not sure, but he didn't say anything else the rest of the way.

Fogdingle Peak is fairly big as mountains go. We drove on a road that curved round and round and up and up. It took forty-five minutes to get to the top; Sal and Sage and I sat in the back and didn't speak. We looked out the window and occasionally looked at each other. We knew what we were all thinking: somebody *owns* this mountain. I don't think any of us felt comfortable meeting that somebody. When we reached the top and got out the air was noticeably cooler than it had been below. Partly this was because it was now dusk, partly it was because we were so high.

It was like another world. You could look down on other mountains not too far off; the rest of the world was way, way below. This must be what the earth looks like to angels, I thought. Each rock and shrub and tree seemed to be lit from within. The changing light of the setting sun made everything magical. The grass had a warm-looking glow but when you reached down it was wet and cool.

Mr. Fogdingle's home was as big as a city block. It wasn't a house or even a mansion, more like a fortress with towers and turrets. The front doors were gigantic and as we walked toward them they suddenly opened and out strode this big man – he was over six feet tall – in a riding outfit. His head looked exactly like George Washington's on the quarter, right down to the little ponytail in the back. His hair was completely white but it was thick and he appeared to be robust and strong.

"Welcome, welcome," he shouted and held out his hand. "I'm Ainsworth Fogdingle. And you," he turned to me, "must be Rick Hasselbach." I introduced him to Sage and Sal and he gave each of us a hearty handshake. "Come on in."

As we followed him we glanced at each other and almost laughed. So this was Aunt Polly Esther's fragile old man living on borrowed time.

"You must be hungry," Mr. Fogdingle shouted over his shoulder as he led us down an oak-paneled hallway. His boots rang on the stone-tiled floor. "Had any supper?'

"No," we told him. We pushed through a set of doors and we were in a kitchen about the size of an entire cottage. It was the sort of kitchen a hotel might have, with huge stoves and ovens, all kinds of knives and utensils and pots and pans hanging overhead. Stainless steel sinks and refrigerators and freezers. Barrels and jars filled with God-knows-what. In the middle was a long marble countertop and smaller chopping blocks. Five cooks in freshly laundered white outfits stood ready to spring into action.

"My staff is here to meet your needs," Mr. Fogdingle told us, gesturing to the three men and two women who stood impressively in a group. "Any dish you want, they'll prepare it. They're quite resourceful, if I do say so myself." He smiled at them and on cue they all smiled back.

"So," Mr. Fogdingle said, rubbing his hands together with relish, "What would you like? Something simple? Something fancy? Your wish is their command."

He paused and we stood dumbfounded. We couldn't have ordered a meal to save our lives. I think he knew that, in fact he had planned on it, for he abruptly snapped his fingers and said, "I know what – if I may make a suggestion. When I was a lad and it was evening in the summer at about this time and I had to go to bed, and of course I didn't want to go to bed, no lad does on a summer evening, and back then we had a much earlier curfew than you young people do today, well, when I had to go to bed at about this hour, my mother would say to me, Tom, would you like a glass of milk and a peanut butter sandwich before tucking in? It was our little ritual, but I suspect there are many a boy and girl who have had a similar experience and who know that on a summer evening at about this hour, nothing tastes so good as a glass of milk and a peanut butter sandwich.

"Now I know you're tired after your long journey," he reassured me, putting his arm around me in a grandfatherly manner. "I have no intention of suggesting you make the peanut butter sandwiches. What kind of host asks his guests to prepare their own meal? I'm sure my staff here is quite up to the task. I doubt they will prepare anything equal to what you are capable of, but what they prepare will be quite serviceable.

"So what do you say? Shall it be peanut butter and jelly with milk?"

"Sure, that would be great," I said. "But I'd be happy to make the sandwiches. It's no work at all, really. Not that your own chefs wouldn't do an excellent job. Anybody can make a peanut butter and jelly sandwich."

Mr. Fogdingle laughed a great laugh. "I like that. A lad with a sense of humor. Well, if you are sure it won't be an imposition. I realize I only contracted for lunch."

"I'd be happy to," I repeated. Immediately he dismissed his staff with a short nod of the head. They walked out together. I don't think they had really expected to prepare a meal.

Mr. Fogdingle rubbed his hands together once more. "Well, well, peanut butter and jelly sandwiches it is." He walked over to one of the giant steel refrigerators and opened it. "Here's the peanut butter," he lifted it out and set it on the counter, "and we have any number of jellies: grape, strawberry, peach, raspberry, loganberry, boysenberry, marmalade.... Grape's my own favorite, but don't let me impose my tastes on you. They're all perfectly serviceable. My fondness for grape is a purely sentimental attachment. It brings back memories of summer evenings at about this hour and my dear mother. She always made my sandwiches with grape jelly."

"Grape would be fine," I told him.

"Grape it is, then!" He pulled out a jar of Jiff and a jar of jelly and put them on the long counter, then he fetched a loaf of sliced white bread. He stood back to give me space to work.

I think he expected some kind of performance. After I made the sandwiches I looked up and saw disappointment in his face. There was nothing out of the ordinary in what I did. He had flown me in on his private jet and had waited for me as if he were a kid again and I was Santa Claus and all I had done was slop some peanut butter and jelly onto some slices of bread. I handed him two sandwiches on a plate.

He stared at them with a defeated expression and for a while I thought he wasn't going to eat. He picked one up and took a bite, chewed it slowly, paused for a moment, chewed again, swallowed. He paused again, as if considering something. Then he wolfed down the rest of the sandwich. He took the second and this one he ate more deliberately, savoring each bite. He drank his glass of milk in a single gulp.

He stood for what seemed like a long while not saying a word. He sat down slowly with a faraway gaze. He turned to me and put his hand on mine. "Boy, that's a gift you've got in those hands, a God-given gift. I watched you do it but I don't know how you do it. It's a miracle."

He cleared his throat. "But listen to me go on and you folks tired and hungry. Please sit down and eat. I don't know what came over me. My parents did teach me table manners."

We sat down and started to eat and Mr. Fogdingle seemed to recover his self-possession. He once again became the genial host.

"It's good to have you here." He slapped his hand on the table. "Seems the only time I see people here is for business. I think my secretary explained my problem to you. It's this blood pressure thing. Very strange. Doctors tell me I require thin air. I can only live on a mountain top. They explained the chemistry of it, but it went in one ear and out the other. The long and the short of it is, I leave this mountain I have to go to a mountain this far above sea level. I go down a thousand feet and my ticker explodes. I can't go into the world so the world has to come to me, at least that part of the world that wants to do business with me."

He snorted.

"That's all the people I see, people with business on their minds. Sometimes that's a lot of people so I had to build premises to accommodate them. The thing is, when I'm not doing business I rattle around here like a pea in a ship's hold. I'm the only man in the world who built and paid for his own prison. My crime: bad blood pressure."

He shook his head. "Oh, I have my diversions. I've got my music, my books, my gardens. I've got a movie screen in a projection room. It's odd though, watching a movie by yourself. It's not like watching TV. Just you and the big screen. You hear someone laugh and you say to yourself, who's that joker? Then you realize. It's you."

We had finished eating and were sitting at the counter listening to him. I have to say, I liked him. For a guy who lived in the clouds he came across as down-to-earth.

"Tell you what," he said. "Tomorrow morning I'll give you the grand tour. But now, I can see, you're tired. You've come a mile or two to get here. Robert will show you to your rooms. Get a good night's sleep and we'll meet in the dining room for breakfast. Eight o'clock sharp. One thing I can't abide, it's a wasted day."

When he said that I thought of Aunt Polly Esther and I had to smile.

The grand tour turned out to be pretty grand. Mr. Fogdingle's premises are difficult to describe if you haven't been there. Imagine Camelot but then imagine King Arthur is the head of a huge corporation – actually a whole kingdom of corporations. There's a Round

Table, a big one, but guys in suits not guys in armor sit around it. There aren't medieval weapons – spiked balls or lances or broadswords – on display, but state-of-the-art telecommunications technology. No guards in colored tights, just security cameras. But the halls are made of stone and the ceilings are built out of carved wood. There is an outer wall with turret-like towers, but the turrets are actually reception dishes.

Most of the time King Fogdingle's knights were out in the world doing what modern knights do. (I don't have a clue myself.) The king meanwhile was at home without even a Guinevere to keep him company. It sounds a little silly the way I'm telling it but there was nothing silly about T. Ainsworth Fogdingle except his name. As we were strolling through his gardens and he was identifying various shrubs and flowers (he seemed prouder of his gardens than he was of his corporations) I worked up the courage to ask him about that name.

"Sir," I began. He was the sort of man you just naturally addressed as sir, the way you would address a king as sire. "Sir, I hope this isn't rude, but I have to say you don't seem at all like your name."

"Really. What image does the name Ainsworth Fogdingle call up in your mind? If you don't mind my asking."

"Well,' I said, considering, "I'm not sure exactly. I think I would know him if I saw him. I don't think he would look anything like you."

He laughed and clapped me on the back. "Dammit, boy, I wish you were older. I'd bring you on board like that!" He snapped his fingers. "You're right. I'm not T. Ainsworth Fogdingle. My God-given name was Tom Peppercorn. When I was a young man starting out I changed it.

"It was after a bad patch when I had lost all of my money, what little I had. I felt I was a terrible failure. I wanted to leave my old self behind, become a new man. I started with my name. Tom Peppercorn, I said, is a name that will never be taken seriously in the business world. At the time I was reading a novel in which there was a rich and powerful man named Ainsworth Fogdingle. I added the T. for Tom as a reminder of my old handle." He grinned and shook his head. "And now that I think about it, that character wasn't anything like me."

"Do you feel that name made you different in any way?" Sal asked him.

He thought about that for a while. We continued to walk through the garden.

"I guess I don't have an answer to your question, Sally," he said at last. "I know I'm not the boy I used to be. A lot of that is age and experience. Did the name help?" He considered some more. "It might just have been my way of giving myself permission to imagine possibilities. Growing up in the Great Depression as I did, that wasn't easy to do. As I said, I'd lost everything. Make-believe was all I had."

"But at least you were able to choose your name," I said. "My name is Richard Wolfgang Hasselbach. Why Richard? Because there was a great composer named Richard – Richard Strauss – and a great physicist – Richard Feynman. Why Wolfgang? Because of Mozart and a scientist named Wolfgang Pauli, who was one of the guys who invented quantum mechanics. Before I was even born my folks were arguing whether I would be a scientist or a composer. So they loaded all these dead people onto me – their idea of a compromise – and I've got them with me for the rest of my life.

"I wish I was an Indian, a Dakota or something like that. If you were a Dakota they at least had to wait until they had some clue who you were before they gave you a name. Then they would know what to call me. Dances With Peanut Butter maybe. I'd prefer that to Richard Wolfgang Hasselbach."

"It sounds like your folks expect a lot from you," Mr. Peppercorn said. "That's not entirely bad."

"But they don't spend any time with me. If they paid any attention to me it would be obvious I can never become what they want me to be. They're totally into their own careers."

"Rick," he said, "you've put your finger on the nub of it. When I was a little older than you, I made up my mind that I wanted to be a rich and powerful man. I knew I wouldn't have time for a family, so I didn't have one. I have men under me now who are just as ambitious as I was but they have families. At least they think they do. Myself, I'm not so sure. They don't spend much time with them."

He turned to Sage. "You've got an unusual name, young man. Is it one you gave yourself?"

"Oh no," he said. "My parents gave it to me. Sagittarius Millennium Faulkner. Sagittarius is a centaur, the top half a man, the bottom half a horse. The bottom half has four feet planted on the ground. The top half, the man, draws a bow and aims his arrow at the sky. My parents wanted me to be grounded but to be an idealist who shoots for the stars. Sagittarius is supposed to represent creative tension. He's also lucky, he reaches his goal despites the odds. I like my name. I hope it suits me."

"It is strange though. Has it given you any difficulties? In school, perhaps?"

"I was home schooled," Sagittarius said. "In college it didn't matter so much. It has been a problem on job applications. Employers often see it as a red flag. And they may be right. I've always been something of a maverick."

"Home schooled. Your parents must have devoted a lot of their time to you."

"Oh yes."

"In our negotiations to bring you here," Mr. Peppercorn said, "we dealt with a Ms. Polly Esther Potter. What is her role? She seemed to have determinative authority."

"That's Aunt Polly Esther," I told him. "She's my mother's sister. She's really the one who looks after us." I nodded toward Sal. "Sal's parents work on her estate. Sagittarius works for her too. He's our tutor."

"She has an estate?"

"Sort of. She runs it as a bed-and-breakfast in the summer."

"Hmm." You could tell this didn't quite make sense to him. I wasn't about to tell him she called her estate Mildew Manor. "Her real job is writing fiction. She's the most successful fiction writer in the country."

"Hmm. I've never heard of her. Maybe you could jot down a couple of her titles before you leave."

I don't think so, I thought.

As we continued to walk along Mr. Peppercorn seemed lost in thought.

"I don't know," he mused. "It's hard. I decided to give up a family and go for success. But here I am with my success at the top of a mountain and no one to share it with. No one to give my name to. And as Rick rightly points out, it's not even my name. It's the name of a man who never existed."

I was sorry now that I had brought the subject up. I didn't want him to feel bad but I needed to do one more thing to put this name business behind us.

"Sir, could I ask a favor of you? Somehow I can't think of you as T. Ainsworth Fogdingle and now that I know it isn't your real name it just feels too weird calling you Mr. Fogdingle. Would you mind much if I called you Mr. Peppercorn?"

"I'd feel more comfortable with that name myself, sir," Sagittarius added.

"Me too," Sal put in.

He thought a moment and nodded. The change seemed agreeable to him. "Mr. Peppercorn it is."

Our tour was over and it was time for lunch. Mr. Peppercorn proposed that we pack some peanut butter sandwiches and have a picnic.

"There are some mighty beautiful prospects on this mountain. You couldn't ask for better weather than we have today."

I made sandwiches and we packed up and headed out. Mr. Peppercorn led us to an outcropping that seemed to overlook the edge of the world. It was almost as if we were astronauts, it was that beautiful. We didn't say much at first, just made small talk. Mr. Peppercorn started asking us about our interests, our plans for the future. Sagittarius said he wanted to teach the way he had been taught. He talked about his experiences as a teacher, how he always got fired when he tried his own ideas.

"I never got the hang of school, myself," Mr. Peppercorn said. "Never figured out how to do what they wanted me to do. My teachers got pretty exasperated, but it wasn't like I didn't want to learn. I just couldn't seem to learn in a classroom. I never did graduate."

"Did they kick you out?" Sal asked.

"I kicked myself out," Mr. Peppercorn said. "It was best for all concerned. I failed at school, I said, but I will not fail at life."

He reflected a moment, then he asked Sage, "What sort of school would you find congenial? As a teacher, I mean."

"The same kind of school I'd find congenial as a student. I've thought a lot about my ideal school. It would be named after Ralph Waldo Emerson and would be based on Emerson's philosophy of life. Its motto would be, 'Always do what you are afraid to do.'"

Mr. Peppercorn chuckled. "I like that! 'Always do what you are afraid to do.' That's the principle upon which I've built Fogdingle Enterprises, though I've never put it that way. So Emerson said that?"

"Well, actually it was his Aunt Mary Moody Emerson," Sagittarius said. "But he remembered it and lived his life accordingly."

"This school of yours then would be named after Emerson and run according to his wisdom?"

"Yes, sir."

"It seems peculiar, though," Mr. Peppercorn went on. "Making a school a shrine to a dead man. 'The persons who make up the world today, next year die, and their experience dies with them.' I believe Emerson wrote that in his essay, 'Self Reliance.'"

Sage suddenly looked at Mr. Peppercorn with new respect. "You've read Emerson?"

"There's not a whole lot to do up here *but* read and tend my roses. And yes, Emerson is one of those writers I dip into now and again. I was a poor student but I did love to read. Still do."

He turned to Sal. "And you, young lady. If you were to act upon this principle of Emerson's, if you did what you are afraid to do, what would you do?"

Sal looked at Mr. Peppercorn, then looked down at her hands. She didn't say anything. Mr. Peppercorn waited.

"What do you mean?" she asked.

"I'm asking you what your secret fantasy is. Not," he held up a finger, "not a daydream you've shared with your friends here, but the daydream you haven't told them. The daydream you are afraid to tell anyone. Will you tell me that daydream?"

Again she didn't say anything and again Mr. Peppercorn waited. I had to rescue her.

"Sal is very shy, Mr. Peppercorn."

"It's silly," Sal said.

Mr. Peppercorn nodded.

"It's dumb."

"Yes."

Sal took a breath. "A singer in a rock band." It rushed out of her.

"Sal!" That was me. Shy, quiet Sal a singer in a rock band? Where did that come from?

"I said it was silly. I said it was dumb." She was blushing a deep red.

"What about you, Rick?" Mr. Peppercorn turned to me. "If you did what you are afraid to do, what would it be?"

Now I was staring at my hands.

"Too silly? Too dumb? Our most secret fantasy usually is."

He waited.

"Well, yeah," I said, "Sure, I have I have a secret fantasy. I mean, it's not like I think it could happen. It's totally unreal. But it's a daydream I have sometimes."

I looked over at Sal. She was still focused on her hands and she was still blushing. I felt sorry for her.

"There's this movie, *Casablanca*, starring Humphrey Bogart and Ingrid Bergman. It's an old black-and-white movie but I really like it. It's about this American named Rick who has his own nightclub in Casablanca. It's during World War II and his club is the most popular place in town. He wears a white dinner jacket and a black bowtie but he never circulates among the customers. He sits alone, playing chess against himself and drinking champagne; sometimes he signs checks to cover bets at the roulette tables. There are all kinds of interesting people at his place, but he's the most interesting because he doesn't let anyone get close to him, so of course they're fascinated. Who is he? He used to be an idealist but he fell in love with a woman who broke his heart and now he's pretty much a cynic. He's like the coolest guy in school, too cool for any clique. He doesn't care what anyone else thinks of him. 'I stick my neck out for nobody.'" I said that in my fake Bogart voice.

"Sometimes I imagine I have my own club where all the terrific bands and singers want to perform and everybody comes there. I wear a white dinner jacket and drink champagne and sign checks to cover the bets. It's pretty dumb, I'll admit."

"Yes it is," Sal said. But she was grinning and she wasn't blushing anymore.

"Would your club have to be in Casablanca?" Mr. Peppercorn asked.

I thought for a moment. "No, I guess not," I said. "But in my fantasy it's in a foreign city. Some place where being an American would make you interesting."

"And Ingrid Bergman?"

"Ingrid Bergman?"

"Is there an Ingrid Bergman in your fantasy?"

"Oh well…I don't know." Now I was blushing. Mr. Peppercorn reached over and tousled my hair. "Just teasing."

We were quiet for a while and took in the scene before us. I thought about what Mr. Peppercorn had said about how he had no family, no one to whom he could give his name or fortune. He had reached the pinnacle of success, literally, but his success had become a lonely prison. He may have had similar thoughts.

"I think that was the best time in my life," he mused, "when I was young and had nothing but impossible hopes. Don't believe what we old people tell you. When you're young, anything is possible. Anything. That's how I felt when I was your age, son," he said to Sage. "I was a soldier in the American army that liberated Paris. You've probably seen the newsreels, the GIs on top of tanks rolling through the city, the crowds cheering. I didn't really experience that. I was too far back. By the time I got to Paris the party was pretty much over.

"I was walking through one of those narrow streets they have and I stopped in front of what looked like a bombed-out restaurant. It was dark inside but way in the back there was a man standing at a stove cooking something. I was curious so I strolled in to take a closer look. This fellow was not much more than a youngster. He was dressed in rags, but his hands were clean and he was holding a pan full of eggs.

"'An omelet,' he told me. 'Want some?'"

"It smelled delicious and I couldn't recall the last time I'd eaten, so I accepted his offer. He found two plates and divided the omelet in half. We took our plates out into the air. As we ate I told him my story and he told me his. He had been a baker's apprentice and then joined the French underground toward the end of the war. There were times he had to live on grasses and roots in the forest. He was skinny as a rail. He promised himself that as soon as Paris was liberated he would come back to the city and make himself an omelet. When things were really bad that thought was what kept him going, cooking and eating an omelet in Paris. That was his impossible fantasy.

"We became close friends and after I returned to the States we kept in touch. We both became successful men, busy men, so we didn't spend as much time together as we would have liked. But whenever I was in Europe I made a point of having a meal with him in his restaurant." He paused. "I can't do that anymore."

"Does he still have his restaurant?" Sage asked.

"Oh yes. It's called *Champ des Fraises*."

"*Champ des Fraises*? Your friend is Louis Duval?" I'd never seen Sagittarius so excited.

Mr. Peppercorn nodded.

"Who is Louis Duval?" Sal and I asked.

"Duval is one of the great chefs of Europe," Sage said. "When I was in college I took a year off to travel in Europe and I ended up in Paris. When I was there, I heard this amazing story about him. *Champ des Fraises* means Field of Strawberries. His restaurant is famous for its strawberry desserts. It was a favorite restaurant of the

Beatles; they used to go there all the time. One evening they were gabbing with Louis Duval after the restaurant had closed and got onto the subject of most-hated foods, foods you couldn't choke down even if someone put a gun to your head. Ringo's most-hated food was rutabagas and this night he went on and on about rutabagas, doing hilarious riffs about how toxic and truly awful rutabagas are. He had everyone rolling on the floor with laughter.

"The Beatles had to fly out of Paris the next day late in the afternoon. Louis Duval said that they should drop by for lunch before taking off. It cramped their schedule a bit but Duval was a good friend so they agreed. They show up for lunch the next day and Duval says he has prepared something special for them. His waiters bring out a soufflé and they serve a portion to Paul and John and George and Ringo. A little salad and a modest white wine. The Beatles love it. You've outdone yourself, Louis, they tell him. This is inspired.

"I'm so touched that you like it, Duval tells them. It's a new creation, invented just this morning. I'm calling it soufflé Ringo and I'm putting it on the menu.

"Ringo is bowled over. 'I suppose you can't reveal the ingredients,' he says.

"'Not at all.' says Duval. "There is nothing secret about the ingredients of this soufflé. It's made of eggs and fresh rutabagas.'"

We all laughed even though we had seen the punch line coming.

"But that's not the best part," Sage broke in. "That's not why this story is a legend in Paris. The Beatles finish their lunch, leave, go back to their hotel and cancel their flight. They're going to stay one more day and write a song to honor Louis Duval. They stay up all night writing it and at five in the morning they go to his home and stand in the street under his bedroom window and serenade him with, that's right, 'Strawberry Fields Forever.'

"They wake up Louis but they also wake up Louis' neighbors,

none of whom realizes that these are the Beatles. One of them calls the police. The police arrive, it all gets sorted out, and the neighbors are mortified that they almost had the Beatles arrested. No sweat, say the Beatles. An impromptu block party develops, the Beatles playing and Duval and his neighbors dancing. Then everyone, including the police, go to *Champ des Fraises* for a strawberry breakfast."

When he finished I didn't know what to say. The story was too fantastical to be true. But I knew it was true.

"Is Louis Duval really that good," I asked Sagittarius.

"In France," he said, "he's considered the Picasso of haute cuisine. He does everything but his specialties are desserts," Sagittarius looked over to Mr. Peppercorn, "and omelets."

"Those eggs I ate with him in '45 were the best meal I'd ever eaten," Mr. Peppercorn said. "Until you came."

Our visit to Peppercorn Peak (I just don't like that word Fogdingle) stretched into a week. We watched our favorite movies in Mr. Peppercorn's private theater and hiked around on the top of the mountain. We spent lots of time talking with Mr. Peppercorn. He had lived an incredibly interesting life and had plenty of stories to tell.

When we left we felt we were abandoning him. It was sad but we had to go. On the last day he asked what my fee would be. That week on the mountain and all his stories were payment enough, I told him. He accepted this but added, "I remain in your debt."

We promised to write, climbed into the van that had brought us, and rode back down.

CHAPTER 4

When we got back to Chicago, summer was just about over and school was starting up again. I got caught up in soccer and homework with Sage and I guess I didn't communicate with Mr. Peppercorn as often as I might have. Sal, though, e-mailed him faithfully.

At Christmas, Mr. Peppercorn sent us presents: four roundtrip airline tickets to Paris. The fourth ticket, he noted, was for Aunt Polly Esther. "From what you told me about her during your visit to Fogdingle Peak, I suspect she may wish to accompany you." We were booked to depart on June 11th, right after school was over, and to return August 25th. Mr. Peppercorn said his friend Louis Duval had arranged for free accommodations for us during our stay.

It wasn't difficult to persuade my parents and Sal's parents to let us go. They saw it as a great opportunity. My dad immediately arranged a visit for me to a physics lab in Paris and my mother worked up an itinerary of musical performances for me to attend. The problem here was too much enthusiasm. Aunt Polly Esther, it turned out, was the one who needed to be persuaded. "Summer is the high season for Mildew Manor," she huffed. "How could I abandon my guests? Who would prepare breakfast for them? Who would see that they made their beds and picked up their rooms?" It was a long phone call from Mr. Peppercorn that convinced her. He must have played up his heart ailment – a dying man's wish and all that. Whatever it was, she agreed to go. And I agreed to visit the physics lab and go to some concerts. One or two.

Aunt Polly Esther took care of the business of passports while Sage insisted we start learning about France before going over. He even started teaching us the language. He was fluent in French, from his time in Paris, I guess. All of which was fine with Sal, but learning a language just to go on vacation didn't make sense to me. "Remember what Emerson wrote," I told Sage. "'Traveling is a fool's paradise.' Also, 'Traveling is a symptom of a deep unsoundness.'"

He replied, "He also wrote in the essay you've been quoting, 'Do that which is assigned to you and you cannot hope too much or dare too much.'"

It was no good trying to get round Sage with Ralph Waldo Emerson.

Finally it was June 11 and we had checked in our bags, gone through security and were waiting to board. It was kind of exciting, actually. I had never flown across an ocean or been to a foreign country. In less than half a day we would be in a country where most people didn't speak English. A high school French class, thirteen girls and two guys, was also booked on our flight; the girls were giggling and the guys pretended to be cool.

"Hey, I just realized," Sal said to Aunt Polly Esther, "you can gather material for a new diet book."

"You don't think I haven't already thought of that?" Aunt Polly Esther snorted. "I've already got my title: *France on 1,500 Calories a Day*."

"Aunt Polly Esther," Sage laughed, "that isn't a diet book, that's a fairy tale."

"If it pans out the way I think it might," she said, "I'll do a whole series. I brought my camera."

The minutes crept by…a delay was announced…the delay was cancelled. Suddenly we were filing onto the airplane. I thought of Mr. Peppercorn and wished he could have come along. We stowed our carry-on stuff overhead and sat four abreast in the middle of the plane. I'd never seen an airplane so big. Hard to believe it would lift off the ground when all the seats were full.

I won't go through the whole eight hours it took to get to Paris. There was some screw-up and they couldn't show in-flight movies, so Sage invented a game to pass the time. It was called "The Memory Peddler". He said a peddler came to a village and went from house to house pulling a cart and crying, "Memories for trade, memories for trade!" You gave him one of your memories and you got someone else's in return. It was one of those round-robin things where each person has to link up with the story that gets passed around as the villagers discover their neighbors' memories of experiences they had shared – or thought they had shared – and also long-kept secrets. Shortly after the flight attendants came through announcing that they would be serving breakfast. It was Sal's turn and she was doing a ghost memory and she started to whisper. All around us voices called out, "Speak up, we can't hear you." Apparently in our section of the plane *we* had been the in-flight movie.

There was the hassle of deplaning, moving through corridors and up and down stairs in a crowd. We waited to get our bags off the luggage carousel, then waited again to go through customs. We pushed through glass doors into an area filled with people who had come to welcome passengers. Aunt Polly Esther exclaimed, "Gracious, who is that?" She pointed to an older man holding up a sign, "Welcome Polly Esther, Sally, Rick, Sagittarius." We struggled through the crowd hauling our heavy bags. When we reached him he smiled a big, warm smile. "Polly Esther Potter?" he inquired in a French accent. She replied, not smiling, "Who are you?"

"I am Louis Duval," he declared. "Welcome to France!" And he kissed her on both her cheeks.

As Monsieur Duval whisked us away from the airport in his red Renault, Aunt Polly Esther's eyes were still glazed over. "It is my pleasure and my honor to be your host in Paris," he was saying as he darted through the murderous traffic. "I hope your stay will be a very happy one. *Malheureusement*, this first day will be difficult. You have just had a long flight on which, I think, you were not able to

Champ des Fraises

sleep much. You wish only to drop into a bed. But this you must not do. No. My friends, there can be no sleep for you on your first day in Paris. You have heard of jet lag? Sleeping in the day, waking at night? A whole week can be spent so if you sleep now, as you wish to. You must wait until it is dark before you go to bed."

Good grief. It was 8:30 a.m. Paris time. We had to stay awake another twelve, thirteen hours? On the other hand, the chances of falling asleep in this car with Monsieur at the wheel were remote, unless it was the sleep of death.

"It is my duty to keep you on the move so you do not sleep." His eyes were on us, our eyes were on the road. I began to repeat the Lord's Prayer in my mind. "For this purpose, I will show you Paris. My Paris. As the English say, a Cook's Tour."

And that is what he proceeded to do, a cook's history of Paris. This history began in 1765, M. Duval informed us, careening into the path of an oncoming semi, with the first 'restaurant' in the city. It took its name from *bouillon restaurant*, which meant meat broth, though the owner served more than meat broth. What made it special was that people were served at individual tables and could choose their meal from a menu.

About twenty-five years later, at the start of the French Revolution, there were a hundred restaurants in Paris and ten years later there were five hundred. All the people who used to cook for aristocrats on their estates were opening their own restaurants, the aristocrats having lost their appetites when they lost their heads. There were so many restaurants that a guy named Alexandro Grimod hired a team of tasters to go around and sample dishes and write up the results, which he published in a book and sold to people who wanted a guide to places to eat.

M. Duval told us a lot of incredible stories. Like how there was a siege of Paris and the poor people ate dogs and cats but the rich could still eat at fancy restaurants where they were served things like elephant consommé, roast camel, kangaroo, rib of bear and haunch of wolf. M. Duval swore this was true. He took us to the biggest market I had ever seen. He took us to eating places that looked like movie sets, places that *had* been movie sets. Places where Hemingway ate, and Scott Fitzgerald, and Greta Garbo and Bob Dylan even. Yeah, Bob Dylan. He would eat at this hotel called George V. Not exactly a counterculture place, believe me.

It was different, I'll say that – seeing a city in terms of food. Definitely not the usual tourist spin. But it was exhausting. By the end of the day, about dinnertime, we were really, really tired. I was ready to hit the floor even if I died of jet lag. That's when M. Duval took us to *Champ des Fraises*. It was a big place, maybe half a block wide and it had class. Brass and wood and gilt mirrors everywhere. Chandeliers that could give you snow blindness if you stared at them too long. The carpet was deep red with a strawberry pattern. It was packed when we got there, waiters rushing around with trays and plates of food.

M. Duval led us to a small private room. "You have been brave," he said. "You have held up better than I expected. The day has been difficult but you are the better for it. Now is your reward. A relaxed meal and then to bed." He smiled. "I have taken the liberty of arranging our menu in advance." He walked over and opened the two windows in the room, letting in the summer air. "Loosen your buttons," he said. Waiters came with the first course.

There is no way I can describe that meal. Maybe people in heaven eat like that all the time. There were seven courses and every single thing was new to me. The more we ate, the more relaxed we got. M. Duval told us about himself and about meeting Mr. Peppercorn while he was cooking those eggs and about the time they spent together in Paris. Mr. Peppercorn used his army connections to get food for M.

Duval and his family when there was very little food in Paris. Mr. Peppercorn – M. Duval called him "Tom" – was practically a member of the Duval family. He told us about meeting his future wife when he was in the Resistance during World War II and their marriage and their two daughters, and about his wife's death two years before.

He asked Aunt Polly Esther what she would like to do during her time in France and she told him about her plan to do a diet book for Americans traveling in France – 1,500 calories a day. M. Duval raised his eyebrows but nodded as if the idea was a plausible one. He asked Aunt Polly Esther why Americans were so enthusiastic about dieting. "Don't they like food?" he inquired innocently. Normally Aunt Polly Ester would have taken offence at this remark but she had had two glasses of wine. (I had never seen her drink an alcoholic beverage before. Was this her first time? I hoped she wasn't going to get tipsy. None of us had had much sleep.) She appeared to have taken a cotton to M.Duval. ("Taken a cotton to" was one of her expressions.) She launched into her ideas about dieting and the American Dream. M. Duval listened raptly, as if she were making sense. Sal came to the rescue, asking M. Duval if Sage's story about the Beatles was true. He chuckled and said, yes, it did happen, but he didn't elaborate. "Those boys could play music," was all he said.

He pursed his lips. "The music today is too loud, much too loud. When I go to a performance of my grandsons I must put something in my ears."

"Your grandsons have a band?" Sal asked.

"Is there a young man who isn't playing drums or a guitar these days? I haven't met him. Jean-Luc and Jean-Michel have been playing together since…always. Now they are very upset. Their singer, she has left them for another band. Love."

Love? Was that some kind of explanation of why the singer left their band? Did she fall out of love with one of them or fall in love with someone else in another band? M. Duval just shrugged, as if the single word love was sufficient explanation.

"How will we find another singer in a week, they ask me. They have a very important – what do you say – a gig? A club is opening. They will play. Without a singer perhaps." He shrugged again. "The music is so loud no one will notice."

"Where is this café?" Sal asked. "Can we go to the opening? I'd love to hear them."

"Of course we will go," M. Duval said. "The café is not far from here. We will drive by it on the way home. Then to bed. It is late, even I am tired. You will sleep in my *maison*." He held up his hand to end our protests. "Yes, yes, my place. I insist. There is no one there now, only me and my housekeeper. Too many empty rooms."

We left by back door and got in the Renault. About ten minutes later M. Duval turned down a side street and pointed out the place where his grandsons would play their gig. A blue canopy came out from what looked like a club. Overhead was a neon sign, but it wasn't lit and I couldn't read it.

CHAPTER 5

We were sitting in M. Duval's kitchen. It was morning and sunlight coming through the windows gave a shine to everything. M. Duval lived in this old, old house made out of stone. It had three floors and many rooms but the rooms were small, even the kitchen, which was cozy and homey like the rest of the house. Our breakfast hadn't been fancy, just milk, coffee, hard rolls, butter and homemade strawberry jam. M. Duval called it a French breakfast. It never changed for the rest of the summer. France doesn't just taste different from America, it smells different. It's not one smell but a lot of smells mixed together. M. Duval's house kitchen had that smell combined with summer morning air. I'd slept through the night with no problems, so I guessed M. Duval had been right. I felt completely at peace.

And then a roaring and a screech exploded outside the house.

"I believe my grandsons have arrived," M. Duval observed with a wry smile.

Two guys came in, one dark-haired, the other blond. They had these European haircuts, the kind that say, we live in Europe, we're cool and sophisticated, we smoke toxic cigarettes.

They kissed M. Duval on both cheeks and he did the same to them. Apparently nobody in France shakes hands or just says "Hi!" M. Duval made the introductions. Jean-Michel was the dark one, Jean-Luc was the blond. Jean-Blond and Jean-Dark, the Euro-Twins. They were a little older than me, but maybe it was just their haircuts that made them look older.

"You're the singer?" Jean-Luc said to Sal.

M. Duval made an exasperated gesture. "Please excuse my grandsons. They are impatient, always in a hurry. They have only a short time to live."

"We only have a couple weeks, Pe′pe′."

"To live?" asked Aunt Polly Esther, shocked.

"Till we perform," Jean-Luc said. He turned back to Sal. "Can you go with us now, Sally? Our practice studio is in Jean-Michel's place."

"Wait a minute," Sal protested. "What are you talking about?"

"It's as I explained last night," M. Duval told her. "My grandsons need a singer if they are to play their gig. When Tom spoke to me" – he meant Mr. Peppercorn – "he said that you were such a singer. Did I misunderstand?"

"I told Mr. Peppercorn it was just a daydream. I've never sung with a band."

"You can't sing?" he said.

"Oh I can sing...."

"Well then?"

"But –"

"Always do what you are afraid to do." I said. "Go ahead, Sally. Do it."

There was a dramatic pause while we all waited.

"Well...I'll come to your studio but I'm not going up on a stage in some club."

"Try, yes," M. Duval clapped his hands. "That's all we ask. Take her away, boys, before she changes her mind."

As quickly as they came the Jeans were gone, taking Sal with them. M. Duval turned his attention to me. "You seem to know very little French. Most young French people speak some English these days, but if you can't use a little French you will not make a good impression."

"Sage tried to teach me French all spring and he didn't get very far," I said. Sage would have definitely backed me up on that but he was still upstairs asleep.

"Yes, He has told me of his efforts to teach you French and he has admitted he was not as successful as he had hoped. But being in

France among so many speakers will make a difference. I think a new teacher will also help. I've taken the liberty of engaging one, a student in her last year at the Sorbonne. She should be here," he glanced at his watch, "very shortly."

"Gee, I don't know," I said. Great. I fly all the way to Paris to stick my nose in a book trying to learn a language I already know I hate.

"It will be easier than you think," M. Duval said. "Danielle will show you Paris and as you discover Paris, you will discover the French language. They are the same, really. Sage tells me that he has given you a basic understanding of the rules. Danielle will take you beyond the rules to something more interesting."

"Who's Danielle?"

"I am Danielle," said a voice behind me, and in turning around I fell off my chair.

She laughed, caught herself, and reached down to help me up. "I'm sorry. It's not funny. I hope you're not hurt." She looked at me with concern. "Oh my. You have been too much in the sun. Is that painful?"

I was totally confused. "He isn't sunburned," Aunt Polly Esther told her. "We just arrived."

Danielle studied me again, then smiled. "I hope this introduction doesn't get us off on the wrong foot – Rick?"

"Yes, ah, I mean no."

"Pardon?"

"Yes, he's Rick, no it's not the wrong foot." This from the always helpful Aunt Polly Esther. I felt like a total idiot.

The idea was for Danielle and me to stroll around Paris together. She would teach me French while we were doing this and at the end of a couple weeks – Bingo! – I would be speaking French. Actually the plan was that she would be my language coach for most of the summer.

tout PARIS av
f PARIS wit
Le Jazz
écouvrez tou S ave
scover all of PA wit
AVENUE GEORGE V
CHAMPS
AV. MONTAIGNE
COURS DE LA REINE
ROND POINT DES CHAMPS ELYSEES
GRAND PALAIS
ULEVARD
SAINT
GERMAIN
ST. GERMAIN DES PRES
R. GUILLAUME APOLLINAIRE
RUE B. PALISSY
RENNES
Transports
en Ile-de-France
Transports
en Ile-de-Fra

That first day we would just get acquainted. She would tell me about herself and I would do the same. She was finishing her work at the university and would graduate in December. She wanted to teach literature in high school – French literature but also literature in English. Her parents were teachers, social science and art. She said that when she was a girl growing up she was very plain. "In English you say 'ugly duckling'? I was an ugly duckling. The other kids called me Danielle Duck." She said the English word for duck.

"I thought *canard* was the French word for duck," I said. A little evidence that I wasn't a complete dunce.

"Very good, Rick! Yes, it is. But they used the English word to be more insulting. Donald Duck was very popular here. My family name is Longdoc. Danielle le Duck was not popular."

I wanted to say to her, boy, you sure aren't ugly anymore. They'd have to call you Danielle la Douce now. Sweet Danielle. I knew the French words but I didn't know her well enough to actually say them. She might get the wrong impression.

I told her about myself. I gave her the short version of my parents and a longer version of Aunt Polly Esther and Mr. Peppercorn and my peanut butter sandwiches. The day was over before I knew it. Boy, did the time go fast. Danielle was a terrific teacher. She'd go from French to English and back again so quickly that sometimes I'd be speaking French without even knowing it. I guess I did make an extra effort to impress her. The conversation never turned into a "French lesson." I have to say that if American students were taught French by Danielle, you'd find a lot more guys lining up to learn the language.

The next day Danielle showed up at M. Duval's wearing trousers and a man's shirt and tie. She had on a man's felt hat, like they wear in old black-and-white movies, her hair tucked under it. She was beautiful in a completely different way than she had been the day before.

"What's this?" said M. Duval when he met her at the door.

"Today I am George Sand," Danielle told him. "Rick and I will see George Sand's Paris. The Paris of Revolution."

"Good," he grunted and sent us off.

We started at the Place de la Concorde, where Louis XVI lost his head. We made our way to the Faubourg Saint-Antoine and the Bastille, where the French Revolution started. It's a district of poor working people where there was another revolution in 1848. The workers put up barricades in the narrow streets and fought with the police. It was the revolution that inspired Victor Hugo's *Les Misérables.* We visited Lenin's flat on Rue Marie-Rose, where he lived for awhile when he was in exile from Russia and was still working through his ideas.

Danielle took me to the Boulevard Saint-Germain, to the cafés associated with Camus and Sartre and Simone de Beauvoir. "Writers are revolutionaries too," she said. "When they change our minds, they change the world." That is why, she claimed, universities must be places where revolution is kept alive. She spoke of the student uprising in Paris in 1968, when students joined with hundreds of thousands of workers and put up barricades and rioted and threw paving stones. The police came in with clubs and tear gas and it was all on television. "Just like in America," she said. She meant the protests over Vietnam that were going on at the same time.

Danielle's personal hero was George Sand, a woman who lived back in the nineteenth century and wrote under a man's name, dressed like a man and smoked cigars.

"You're joking," I said.

"I am not," she shot back and she took a cigar out of her pocket and lit it. She actually smoked it. It was thin, more like a long cigarette, but it definitely smelled like a cigar. She was very serious about George Sand.

"Sand was a socialist, a visionary," she said. "She wrote romantic novels and was very political, like Hugo. All the great Romantics were political. Your own Romantics were very radical – Wordsworth, Shelley, Byron, and the Americans – Emerson, Thoreau, Whitman. The Romantics declared for liberty, equality."

So I got a George Sand tour of Paris. All these famous poets and writers were Sand's lovers. Her books were bestsellers. And all the time she was walking round in men's pants and smoking cigars. Danielle puffed away on her cigars, becoming more like Sand by the minute. American students are apathetic, she declared. They know next to nothing about their own country and nothing at all about Europe or Africa. I got a little defensive, but when she started asking me questions I have to admit I didn't have many answers.

"Are you a feminist?" I finally asked her.

"I am a Romantic," she said. "I am for all people."

For several days we did the arts of Paris. It was easier to speak French because most of our words for the arts come from French, words like symbol and color and painting and sculpture and theater and comedy and tragedy and drama and music and opera and symphony. Often it's practically the same word. I thought we would spend at least one day at the Louvre but Danielle nixed that. She said you could spend a whole day just waiting in line to get into the Louvre, especially in the summer. She arranged with a friend who worked there for us to duck in through a back door, one of those "employees only" entrances. But she set a condition. We could see just two paintings, something I would choose and something she would choose. Then we would leave. "It's too crowded to even see most of the paintings during the summer. Too many tourists."

My choice was the *Mona Lisa*. Not an original pick, I admit, but, hey, I just wanted to be able to say I'd been there and seen it. Did I get to see it? Sort of. I was in large group of people, toward the back. Was I impressed? Not really. I didn't think her smile was all that mysterious. Maybe she was just covering up bad teeth.

Danielle's choice was a huge painting by Eugène Delacroix called "Liberty Leading the People." There was a battle being fought by ordinary citizens in street clothes (though one guy had a top hat on) and a lot of them were already dead. In the middle was this woman with the top of her dress pulled down, exposing her breasts. (I thought that was so French – a big improvement on "Washington Crossing the Delaware.") She was lifting a flag with one hand and holding a rifle and bayonet in the other. Her head was turned and she seemed to be urging the people behind her to keep moving. She was the biggest thing in the picture and she was way more impressive than Mona. I liked Danielle's choice better than mine. And she was right about the crowds. We were out of there.

We went to some other museums; Paris is filled with them. Danielle took me to a theater as well, where people rioted when Stravinsky's *Rites of Spring* was first performed. The people of Paris, apparently, riot at the drop of a hat – a bad king, weird art, you name it, they'll organize a riot. I sent a postcard (in French!) to my folks. One evening Danielle took me to a jazz club where they played very cool jazz. I thought I might try smoking toxic cigarettes. Why not? The second hand smoke was killing me anyway.

The next morning she showed up wearing a black eye patch and announced we would spend the day seeing Dadaist Paris. I had never heard of Dadaists before. According to Danielle they were dedicated to producing anti-art. Marcel Duchamp put a urinal in a museum and signed the name "R. Mutt" to it. Monty Python stuff.

We passed a bakery while Danielle was trying to explain this to me. "Wait," she said and ran inside. She came out with a chocolate pastry. She dipped her finger into the filling and smeared a line of chocolate on either side of my face – a clown's grin. "There," she said, "Now *you* are the Mona Lisa. "She dipped her finger in the chocolate again and drew a mustache over my upper lip. "Now you are Duchamp's Mona Lisa." She put a chocolate mustache on herself. "Me too." When I reached up to wipe the chocolate off my face she grabbed my hand. "No, no. Today we are Dadaists. We will walk through Paris with our chocolate mustaches."

"Danielle," I protested, "You look cute in your mustache, but I don't need a mirror to know I look silly in mine. I don't want to walk around Paris like this."

"Oh but we will," she insisted. "Today we are Dadaists. The new is always silly at first. If you are afraid of being ridiculous you will never be free. Yoko Ono was a Dadaist when she met John Lennon. John Lennon was a Dadaist."

"John Lennon?"

"The Beatles did many Dadaist things. They weren't afraid to be ridiculous."

So there I was with a stupid grin painted on my face walking the streets of Paris with a woman wearing an eye patch and a chocolate mustache. We went to the financial district, the French stock exchange. In the middle of all these guys in suits Danielle would suddenly break into a dumb dance. Or she would go into a Danielle Duck walk and flap her arms. But the crazy part was this: there wasn't a moment when she wasn't beautiful. Even when she was making a complete fool of herself she knocked your socks off.

Every day had a different theme. One day was "Hemingway and friends". Danielle took me to the cafés where all those famous American writers hung out in the Twenties. They practically lived in the cafés, she said, because their apartments and hotel rooms were so small. One day we visited cemeteries for "great stories of Paris." In Père Lachaise I learned about Jim Morrison and Edith Piaf and Oscar Wilde and Eloise and Abelard. By now we were speaking French most of the time. Danielle had a real talent for putting complicated things in simple terms.

The day was overcast and dark. At four o'clock we stopped at a café and Danielle encouraged me to place our order with the waiter. As I thought about the stories she had told me, I realized almost none of them had a happy ending. You could say that's the way life is, but I got the feeling the French *like* sad endings. When I mentioned this to Danielle, she thought a bit, then said, "No, not sad. Bittersweet. Bittersweet endings have more emotions. Americans, I know, want happy endings. I like happy endings. But for Americans happy endings are like Big Macs. It's all they want.

"You're over generalizing, Danielle," I said. "Americans like bittersweet endings too."

"Can you give me an example?"

"Yes I can, my favorite movie. *Casablanca* has a bittersweet ending."

"You're right. *Casablanca* is a wonderful movie and it has a bittersweet ending. It is also a great movie because it has the two classic themes – love and politics. "

"It's a great movie because of Humphrey Bogart and Ingrid Bergman."

"Of course," she conceded. "But actors are nothing without a great story. Love and politics."

"That is so French," I said.

"What do you mean, so French?"

"Sage says that the French are obsessed with love and politics."

She frowned, her eyes on fire. "Sage? Who is this Sage?"

"He's my friend. He came with us. He knows quite a bit about France. He speaks French really well."

"Is Sage a common American name? I've never heard of it."

"It's short for Sagittarius, a one-of-a-kind name." I had to smile. "There's only one Sagittarius." I didn't want to go into the whole thing about Sage's hippy parents. "He's a lot like you, actually, a Dadaist in some ways. I think you'd like him."

"Sagittarius." She studied me for a long moment. "Perhaps you can introduce us and he can teach me about the French and our obsession with love and politics. But does he think only the French fall in love? In movies, Americans go to Paris to fall in love – it's a Hollywood cliché. How sad to have to go to a foreign country to fall in love."

"Good grief, Danielle. Americans don't have to come here to fall in love."

"They do if you believe your movies. American romantic comedies are so shallow. I think Americans do not know what love is. With politics also. Like your Sagittarius, they think these are peculiar French 'obsessions'."

"Danielle –"

"Oh you marry, you vote. You think that is love and politics. But for the French these are passions. Not obsessions. Passions. You have the word but do you know what it means? I don't think so."

"Danielle –"

"I speak of American men. American women, I think they know about passion. But how sad for them because American men do not know. They are tough-guys. They are not able to speak of love. Like Bogie in *Casablanca*. 'I stick my neck out for nobody.' You think that's 'cool'? I think it is sad. Very sad."

"Danielle, I don't think you know what you're talking about. You've based your opinion on Hollywood movies. That's not what Americans are like."

"Oh I know what Americans are like." She was angry now. "When I was about as old as you I met an American, not a movie American but a real man. At least I thought he was real. Now I am not so sure. He was a university student who came to Paris to study for a semester. He rented a room in our house. He was good looking, very romantic. For three months we were close; we shared our ideas. We spoke of liberty, equality. I thought we were soul mates and I fell in love, a stupid French thing to do. He was older than me. In the end he pretended the difference in our ages mattered. He treated me as if I were a child. Oh he was a real tough-guy. I stick my neck out for nobody. Yes."

The way she talked, I wondered if she was still carrying a torch for this guy. "Danielle, we aren't all like that. I'm not a tough-guy."

She took a breath. "No you're not." She recovered her dazzling smile. "You're very sweet. I like you a lot."

"I like you too. You're not Danielle le Duck. You're Danielle la Douce."

"Oh Rick." She lifted her glass of wine and touched my Coke. "Here's looking at you, kid."

CHAPTER 6

It probably sounds like Danielle was with me 24/7 but she had days off. During these breaks I did other things. M. Duval took me back into the kitchens of *Champ des Fraises*. That's right, kitchens – a whole maze of them, each one for a different purpose: "prep kitchens" for vegetables, fish, and meat; a kitchen for the "cold menu," another for the "hot menu," another for receptions and banquets. Walk-in storage rooms and freezers. So many people in motion, it was amazing none of them collided (at least while I was there). It looked like chaos to me but as we edged through M. Duval murmured, "Bon...bon...bon."

I also hung out at the studio of the two Jeans. Jean-Luc played guitar and Jean-Michel played bass. Their drummer, a guy named Marc, hardly said a word but he didn't need to. Everything he wanted to say he could say with his drums. Then there was Sal. She could sing, she had a good voice really, but she didn't give off much energy and she didn't have style. She was too self-conscious. And why wouldn't she be? She'd never worked with musicians before. There was no way for her not to be self-conscious.

I kept imagining how Danielle would be as the band's singer. For all I knew she couldn't carry a tune but she had what Sal didn't – energy and style. She would have been dynamite, no question. It's a rotten thing to do, making comparisons, but that's what I thought as I watched them rehearse. The first time I visited, Sal came over to me during a break and asked, "How are we?"

"Great," I said. "The drummer's incredible."

"I know," she said. Pause. "How was I?"

"You were great."

"That bad, huh?"

"Sal, come on. This is your old confidence problem. You never give yourself enough credit. You've got a good voice. You just need to hone the performance. Work on getting a little more style."

"What do you mean, style?"

"You know. Style. A little more energy. A little more...." I trailed off.

"What should I do? Jump up and down?"

"Sal, that's not what I said."

"I heard what you said. You said I don't have any style."

"No...sure you have style. I didn't say you don't have style. I just said you could work on getting a little *more* style. More energy. That's all."

"That's all, huh?" She was starting to tear up. "Well, maybe what you saw is all I have. If that's not enough, maybe we should ask Danielle to sing. She's got style to burn."

I started to panic. Sal has this capacity to read my mind at times and if this was one of those times we were in serious trouble. "Sal, this is ridiculous. You asked for my opinion and I gave it to you, my honest opinion. I just don't think you've had enough time to reach your full potential."

"You're right," she said. "I'm sorry. It's just that I'm so tense. I can see me making a complete fool of myself in front of a bunch of strangers."

A bunch of strangers? Was Sal really considering performing in a club, in Paris? Not a good idea. "I thought you said you weren't going to perform on stage."

"I don't want to, but Jean-Luc and Jean-Michel are desperate. Their gig is already scheduled. They've wasted all this time with me when they could have been looking for someone else. At this point I'm all they have."

I considered this. "Oh, it's not that big a deal. One gig. It might be exciting. And whatever happens, we're out of here at the end of the summer."

"But Jean-Luc and Jean-Michel won't be out of here. Or Marc. I don't want to let them down."

"You won't. Trust me: performing before a live audience will be a whole different experience."

"I need to go to the bathroom."

That's how it went for the first weeks. I explored Paris with Danielle and Sal rehearsed with the Jeans. I wasn't sure what Sage was doing; I didn't see much of him. And then one morning everything changed. After breakfast M. Duval said I would not be going off with Danielle. "I have a little surprise," he announced. We got into his Renault and headed off. After twenty minutes or so we parked next to the club M. Duval had pointed out that first night in Paris, the club where the Jeans would be performing. We got out. It was 10:00 in the morning and the place had to be closed but M. Duval walked to the door and opened it. No knocking, no key in the lock. He stepped in like he owned the place, with me following. And in one moment everything went *déjà vu*. I had walked into *Casablanca*, the way Dorothy stepped into Oz. The bar, the tables, the lighting – the whole thing was a perfect recreation of the movie set. I almost looked for Humphrey Bogart at one of the tables. M. Duval enjoyed watching my jaw drop. So did Sage, who had suddenly appeared, grinning.

"Not bad, huh?"

"Sage must get much of the credit," M. Duval said. "He has supervised most of the work."

Sage supervised most of the work? What work? I was so confused I didn't know what to say. M. Duval pressed his hand against my back and guided me to the bar where a white dinner jacket was draped. He held it out in front of me. "Put it on," he said, "and let's see if it fits." I stood there dumbfounded. "Come, try it on," he repeated, and helped me into the sleeves. He stood back for an appraisal. "Perfect. What

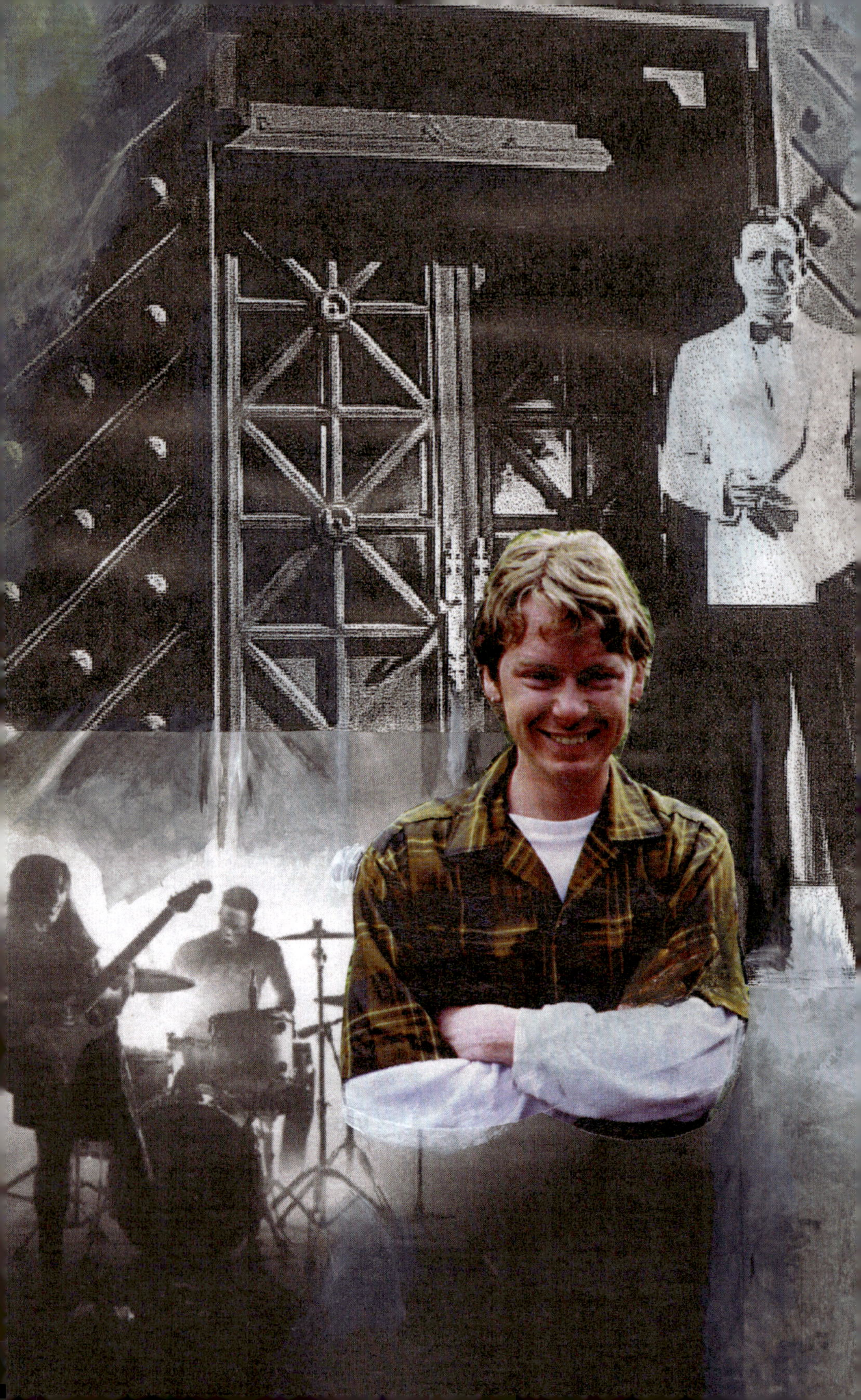

do you think?" he asked Sage. "Perfect," Sage said with a nod. "Aunt Polly Esther got the measurements exactly."

An explanation was in order and it became clear they were bursting to explain. There had been a devious purpose behind Mr. Peppercorn's gift of a free flight to France. He wasn't just sending us off on a vacation. I gradually realized as their explanation unfolded that Mr. Peppercorn intended to realize our most secret wishes: my *Casablanca* fantasy and Sal's dream of singing in a rock band. It was something only a magician – or a very rich and powerful man – could do. But could money alone do it? Mr. Peppercorn could buy or rent a venue in Paris and renovate it to look like a movie set and he could pull some strings with M. Duval to get Sal into a band, but all his wealth and power couldn't buy our success. He could put Sal on a stage with a guitarist, a bass and a drummer, but Mr. Peppercorn couldn't pay audiences to like what they heard. And what about me? Why would Parisians want to go to a café where the host was an American kid in a white dinner jacket who could barely speak their language? Mr. Peppercorn was a highly successful businessman; he knew what it takes to succeed. Hadn't he thought this through? He had wanted to make our dreams come true but he had put us in circumstances where we couldn't possibly succeed. We would pretend to be something we were not – *in public*! – and we would come across as embarrassing phonies. I remembered my conversation with Sal about her performance skills and how I'd compared her in my mind with Danielle. I guess this was God's way of punishing me. I almost winced but the eager faces of M. Duval and Sage stopped me just in time. This was their happy surprise. I had to be happily surprised. I did feel, however, that a few simple questions might be in order:

Q. Will this club serve food and drink?

A. Yes indeed – wine, beer, and soft drinks, as well as coffee. The limited menu will include hamburgers and a variety of American-style sandwiches, though not peanut butter sandwiches.

Q. Will the city of Paris issue a liquor license to a legal minor, a visiting tourist from the US?

A. The liquor license has been issued to M. Duval. Professional French bartenders will serve at the bar. There will be French waiters as well.

Q. Will there be roulette games?

A. No, but some pinball machines will be installed.

Q. What would draw Parisians to such an establishment?

A. *Casablanca* and Humphrey Bogart are still icons in the French imagination.

Curiosity and the association with the famous American movie will be sufficient to draw customers in the short term. And since Rick and Sal and Sage will be returning to the States in late August, a successful Pop-Up restaurant is all we want.

The whole scheme had been carefully thought out, except for its fundamentally ridiculous premise. But I was stuck, for the same reason Sal was stuck. They had invested so much already I couldn't pull out. I thought of my wonderful days with Danielle; I owed it to her as well. If you are afraid of being ridiculous, she had said, you will never be free. Maybe if I just sat quietly in the back of the club sipping my Coke, no one would notice me. Bogart's Rick, after all, had a policy of not interacting with his customers.

Opening night Sal and I were both petrified. She at least was able to sing her songs. I forgot every single word of French I had learned. Dressed in a white dinner jacket and a black bowtie, there was no way I could just disappear in the crowd. When people stared at me I'd just stare back. My eyes started to glaze over.

Apart from my personal humiliation, we had a friendly opening night crowd. They were noisy and out for a good time. Jean-Luc and Jean-Michel had put out the word to all their friends. Sal, I could tell, was feeling the same way I was. Did the audience know? Maybe they thought that her white, stricken face with over-dilated eyes and her immobile body was a new performance style, cool taken to the level of near-death, the latest thing in the States. They applauded enthusiastically after every number. Were they showing Jean-Luc and Jean-Michel that when you are in truly desperate circumstances your friends come through for you big time? Early on, I stopped trying to figure out what was going on. Danielle didn't show and I was so grateful for that small blessing.

At the end of the evening M. Duval clapped me on the back and said, "An immense success."

The next night no one showed up. I don't know if you've ever had an experience like that, standing in the middle of a large, empty room listening to the voice of a frightened singer get smaller and smaller. After each number the waiters standing around applauded politely – clap, clap – a sound that made the emptiness truly awesome. How to explain to someone who has never been there. Time is no longer one minute and then another minute and then another, but just one minute that never ends. If you have never had that experience, friend, then no matter what bad hand life has dealt you, you are blessed.

Wait, I take that back about no one showing up. Occasionally people did wander in because outside there was a canopy and a neon sign – Rick's Café – emblazoned in blue – and they thought there was something going on inside. So they stuck their heads in and then they fled. Every time that happened I thought, "Yes, run. It's too late for me, but you have a chance. Run!"

The next morning Sal and I sat at M. Duval's kitchen table like a pair of zombies. He did his best to cheer us up. "This is typical, believe me, very typical," he said. "A new restaurant, a new café, does not take off over night. It takes time for word-of-mouth to get around."

"M. Duval," I said, "In this case word-of-mouth has moved with lightning speed."

The next four days are a blur. I can't remember them. I was sleepwalking the whole time, maybe because my nights were sleepless. Each evening at the café was the same, except the band stopped going through the pretense of performing. Unfortunately, I had to show up. Sal, God bless her, came every evening and sat with me until the café closed. We shook our heads over the folly of it all. "This was so predictable," I said. "What were M. Duval and Mr. Peppercorn thinking?"

"I'm not sure either of them knows much about club life," Sal reflected. "Probably neither one has been to a club."

"How are the Jeans taking it?"

"They're okay. They don't see it as a judgment on them."

"It isn't. It's a judgment on us."

"I don't think so. I don't think we matter much. I sort of felt invisible opening night. I don't think anyone noticed me."

"I wish I'd been invisible. In this dinner jacket I feel like a performing monkey. A performing monkey without an act."

Sal didn't have anything to say to that. What could she say?

Danielle came one evening. She got a glass of wine at the bar and chatted with me for about an hour, acting as if the silence and emptiness were perfectly normal. She asked how the opening went and then we steered carefully around everything post-opening. She asked how my language skills had fared and I lied and said that I was glad to be able to handle small talk. Gradually our conversation fell into awkward pauses. And then, saying she had another commitment, she got up to go. I stood up to shake her hand and thank her for coming; she leaned over, hugged me, and walked out.

Of all my humiliations, that was the worst.

Finally on the morning of the fifth day M. Duval said, "Today we go into the country. A picnic with my daughters and their families. When it is dark we will shoot off some fireworks. To celebrate your Fourth of July."

The Fourth of July? I guess it was. I had been suspended in an eternity of timelessness. "What about my café, I asked.

"Tonight we close. Every café closes one night a week. You can't work every day."

"M. Duval, I've been thinking. This café was a great idea. It really was. And I appreciate the money and effort you and Mr. Peppercorn put into it. I know what you wanted to happen and I am truly grateful. But I don't think it's going to work. Maybe we should close the café permanently. You could make better use of the space. This must be costing a lot."

"Close down when we've just opened? No, Rick." He put his hand on my hand. M. Duval liked to touch people when he talked to them. "This first week was not good, I admit. Except for the opening, it was very bad. First weeks often are. I won't tell you about the first half year of my restaurant. It would depress you. It depressed me. But if I had closed down, there would be no *Champ des Fraises* today.

"I think Tom told you about how we met, during the war. That was a bad time. You cannot imagine how bad. Every day I faced death and not just my death but the death of my country. France under a Third Reich? For a time it not only looked possible, it looked certain. The end of everything I valued. So please do not speak to me of giving up."

"M. Duval, you said your restaurant did terrible business the first six months."

"More than six."

"But we don't have six months. Sal and I have to fly back to the States at the end of the summer."

"So we don't have six months." He shrugged. "We have next week.

No, we don't close down. Today we go away, we relax. You need to step back and take a breath. We will have a picnic that I will prepare, and I must tell you I am famous for my picnics. Tonight we will have fireworks to celebrate our success next week."

"Our success next week."

"Of course. Unbelievable success. People wait until after success to celebrate, but this is a mistake. When success comes you are too busy to celebrate, so you must celebrate *before*, when you have the time. It makes sense, does it not?"

"No, I don't think so."

But what could I do? He had been too good to us not to go along with him. I added something else to my list of French mysteries that Americans will never understand: love, politics, success.

So off we went. I tried to call Danielle on my cell phone to invite her but it went straight to voice mail. On the ride out to where the picnic would be, M. Duval, Sage, and Aunt Polly Esther jabbered away – the word merrily came to mind – while Sal and I sat quietly. Sal just stared out the window. I think the past week had been harder on her than on me. She has this way of figuring things out so that she's the one at fault. I wanted to comfort her but I didn't know what to say.

After a couple of hours we pulled onto a dirt road that took us to a very old country house. I guess it was a sort of vacation house that was used by all the Duvals. M. Duval's daughters and their husbands and kids and others – uncles, aunts, cousins? – were already there, setting up tables and a volleyball net. We got out, triggering major cheek-kissing. I don't know if you've ever heard a large group of people kissing simultaneously – not deep, silent kisses, but cheek-smacking kisses. It's a sound like no other. The closest thing is a tree full of small birds chirping in the morning. Imagine how that would sound if you were in the tree.

I was surprised how warmly Jean-Luc and Jean-Michel greeted Sal. They took her around and introduced her as if they were showing her off. They weren't just cheering her up. You could tell they really liked her; they seemed proud of her. I suppose their weeks of intensive preparation had been some sort of bonding experience.

M. Duval handled the introductions of Sage, Aunt Polly Esther and me. I was thinking, oh well, it'll be a good occasion to practice my French when M. Duval called out, "Danielle! Over here!" He turned to me. "I invited Danielle." After he introduced her to Aunt Polly Esther and Sage, he took Aunt Polly Esther off to meet his brother, leaving Danielle to chat with Sage and me. She was wearing dark shorts with a white short-sleeved shirt open at the neck.

"Danielle," I said, "I called to invite you myself. Finally you can meet Sage." I turned to Sage. "I've told her a little about you."

"A little?" There was mockery in her voice.

"It's just that I think you could be good friends. You have a lot in common."

"I'm sure," she said and there was still that edge to her voice as she turned on Sage. "I understand you are very informed about the French."

Sage blushed. "Not really."

"But Rick tells me you understand our obsession with love and politics. It's so rare to meet an American who understands these things. I'm very interested in your view."

Right then Duval rushed up and dragged us off to a volleyball game that was just beginning. Good thing too, because Danielle's introduction to Sage was not going well.

The Duval family is very serious about volleyball. Probably it's another of those traditions that go back centuries. Anyway, they compete with a take-no-prisoners intensity. I never got up to their speed but Danielle did. She was on my team and Sage was on the other. She was one of our stars, great on the serve and also at the net. I hadn't seen this side of Danielle, the predator side. I mean, she really wanted to win. One time at the net she spiked the ball down on Sage so hard we thought he might have gotten a black eye. At first she laughed this devilish laugh, then when people were checking his eye she said, "Oh, I'm sorry." It was nothing and Sage stayed in the game. "I really am sorry," she told him, but she didn't sound all that sorry.

The food was terrific. Of course it would be, prepared by a great chef. We sat at long tables eating and talking. The French have a way of stretching out a meal, savoring every minute. At one point I realized I had been talking in French with people I had never met before. Around seven o'clock the sky turned dark with a storm rolling in. There would be no fireworks after all. Not a good omen, I thought. We barely got all the food inside the house when the sky opened up and the rain came down hard.

Right away the Duval Follies were organized, another family tradition. Songs, standup comedy, skits; men played women's parts, women played men's parts. They had a closet filled with hats and accessories and props. I got the impression that some of the jokes and songs had been repeated many times before but they still got an enthusiastic audience response.

Then Jean-Michel introduced Sal. They hadn't brought their guitars, he said, so she would sing solo, without accompaniment. Sal perched on a stool with the Duvals seated around her, some of them on the floor. They had welcomed her into their family and she seemed at ease, happy to be there. She began to sing a ballad I'd never heard before in a country western style. She didn't perform it so much as deliver it straight from her heart, simple and clear.

Crazy
I'm crazy for feelin' so lonely
I'm crazy
Crazy for feelin' so blue

I knew
You'd love me as long as you wanted
And then someday
You'd leave me for somebody new

Worry
Why do I let myself worry
Wondrin'
What in the world did I do

Crazy
For thinkin' that my love could hold you
I'm crazy for tryin'
And crazy for cryin'
And I'm crazy for lovin' you

There was a moment of stillness, as if she had cast a spell, then everyone applauded enthusiastically. Sal grinned unselfconsciously. Probably for the first time in her life she had taken control of an audience. She looked over at me and I gave her a thumbs-up.

None of the Duvals was ready to follow that act so Danielle volunteered. She did a parody of Marlene Dietrich, singing a French torch song with a heavy German accent, really vamping it up. She was wearing shorts, as I said. She stretched forward, one leg lifted onto a chair, a top hat tilted over her eye. The voice, the legs, were perfect. When she finished she got a rowdy response of clapping and whistling. Only Sal, I noticed, was not caught up in her performance. She stared at Danielle in a way that was hard to read.

It was late when we climbed into M. Duval's Renault and started back to Paris. The rain had stopped and the air was clear. I thought about the difference between the boisterous fun of the Duval Follies and the empty café with a few waiters standing at the side making sad clapping sounds. M. Duval had it wrong. Celebrating before you succeed only makes not succeeding that much worse.

CHAPTER 7

When I showed up at the club at 7:00 the next evening I was greeted not with the desolate emptiness I expected but with a totally packed audience buzzing with excitement. On a screen at the back of the stage a video projected scenes from an old newsreel of tanks entering what looked to be Paris. A vocalist on stage belted out a song I didn't recognize at the top of her lungs. She looked to be twice my age and at least twice my size.

The café crowd was going bonkers. Even Sage was there. I cut over to where he stood by himself near the back.

"Hey, what's going on?

"They're what's going on." He nodded toward the stage.

"Who are *they*?"

"They're Rattle Yer Jewelry. I wouldn't be surprised if M Duval pulled some strings and arranged to have them show up. They're currently on tour."

"Who's the amazon?"

"Brynhild."

"Brynhild? What kind of name is that?

"It's Swedish. Brynhild Svendkind."

A blank stare from me.

"Brynhild Svendkind. She's the sister of Lars Svendkind, the guy on the guitar. You don't know about this group? *Devices? Rainbow Machine?* They took home four Grammys last year. You really don't know who they are? Seriously?"

I shrugged. "I'm not into Scandinavian music."

Sage laughed. He thought I'd told a joke.

I was rescued from my embarrassment by Brynhild's brother who stepped to the mic and announced, "We'll be taking a break for an hour to find some of the famous Paris food we enjoyed the last time we were here. But stick around for Dirty Laundry, They're going to rock your faces off. " He waved and Rattle Yer Jewelry left the stage amid thunderous applause.

After what seemed like a minute but was closer to twenty, Dirty Laundry hit the stage.

Sal stepped up to the mic. Oh my god, I said to myself. Sal is going to follow Brynhild the Amazon? My heart went out to her. But I quickly realized she didn't need my pity. She began to speak fluent French with complete confidence, too quickly for me to follow. I think she was thanking Rattle Yer Jewlery.

She launched into her first song and the next fifteen minutes she was on the same wavelength with the audience. Did they realize she was an American minor? She started moving her body in ways totally new to me. How to describe it. Provocative? Yeah, provocative. Her voice and her body were letting folks know, get ready, there's a new show in town.

I relaxed and gradually let myself enjoy her performance – and the band's. They were really good. The rest of their set built on the energy that Rattle Yer Jewery had created.

The next morning I came down to find Sal eating a French breakfast with M Duval. I pulled up a chair and joined them. "You were very impressive last night," I told Sal. "You really connected with the audience."

"I felt the connection," she said." I got some good performance tips from Rattle Yer Jewelry.

"It sounds like you're friendly with the Swedes. Sage seems to be impressed by them. He says they're on tour."

"So why are they playing at a pop-up club like Rick's café? "

"The pressures of the big venues were getting to them. Every night a new city. That can be rough. They'll be going to the States in the fall. They asked me about Chicago."

"Maybe they'll take you along. You and Byrnhild would make an interesting pair of lead singers."

Sal frowned at my sarcasm.

"Sounds like you're jealous, Rick. Brynhild is coaching me on my stage presence.

You were right when you said I needed more energy. The crowd feeds off the lead singer's energy. It can drive them crazy. Just spending time with Brynhild I'm learning a ton."

"What about the Euro-twins. What are they learning?"

"They have names, Rick. And yes, they're learning a lot too. But they're not arrogant about it. They realize what an opportunity this is."

M Duval had been quietly monitoring this conversation, if you can call it a conversation.

He decided to speak up.

"Sally's right, Rick."

"Are you familiar with this group?" I asked him skeptically.

"Sort of. The kitchen crew always have them playing. It's not my kind of music, but I know they're popular with young people."

"Am I the only young person who's clueless about this Rattle Yer Jewelry," I asked in exasperation.

"Ask Sage to bring you up you speed, Ricky. He's your teacher. He lived for a year in Paris. I'm sure he knows all about them."

Ricky. Thanks, Sal.

"They're famous but they don't act like big shots. They asked Dirty Laundry if we'd be interested coming with them as a warm up band. Jean-luc and Jean-Michel are totally on board."

"Sal, have you forgotten? We're going home next month."

"Plans change, Rick. This is an opportunity of a lifetime. A dream come true."

I flashed back to our day with Tom Peppercorn on his mountain when he asked each of us what our secret fantasy was and Sally confessed that her secret wish was to be a singer in a rock band. She was shy about admitting it. She wasn't very shy now.

"What will happen to Rick's Café without its house band?" I asked and glanced at M Duval. He didn't say anything. Had Jean-Luc and Jean-Michel discussed this with him?

"It's like I said, plans can change," Sal said. " We can wait until you've closed Rick's Café. "

A change of plans. Like when the tanks roll into Paris?

CHAPTER 8

"Tom tells me you make an extraordinary sandwich." M. Duval and I were sitting alone at breakfast. Mornings were the only time we had together most days because his workday started about 11:30.

"It's a peanut butter and jelly sandwich," I said. The subject hadn't come up before this and I had hoped it never would. "They're an acquired taste, an American thing. You need to be introduced to them when you're a kid."

"Surely it's not too late to introduce me."

"I don't think you'd really care for them," I said.

"But in the month you've been here you have been introduced to many dishes you had not eaten before. You seem to have enjoyed them."

"I have! But you're a terrific cook...I mean, chef. These things I make are just sandwiches. I'd be embarrassed to give you one."

"Tom tells me something very different. He calls them a miracle. I would be very disappointed not to taste one."

A miracle? Oh brother. But there was no way out. I had to make a peanut butter sandwich for one of the great chefs of Europe.

Which turned out to be a lot less simple than it is in the States. Simply the words "peanut butter" produced baffled frowns on clerks. When I tried to explain what it was they more often than not led me to a spread called Nutella that seemed to be fairly popular. Finding a prepackaged loaf of sliced, squishy, white bread cranked out in an industrial bakery was likewise impossible. The French take their bread very seriously, and so far as I could tell it is seldom sliced and never squishy. I was about ready to give up when Danielle came to the rescue. She suggested I try a small specialty shop that catered to American expats on Rue du Bat, around the corner from the Musée d'Orsay. It had everything I needed. I hauled the ingredients back to

M. Duval's place, slapped them together and handed M. Duval, the Picasso of French cuisine, a peanut butter and jelly sandwich.

Was I tense as he lifted the sandwich to his mouth? Not in the slightest. I felt relieved. I knew he would suppress his gag reflex, choke the first bite down, set the rest of the sandwich back on the plate and then search for something to say that was not dishonest. It would not be easy, I knew, because when it came to food, M. Duval was totally honest. He had to be. In a way I felt sorry for him, but he had brought this on himself by insisting on eating one of my sandwiches. It would be awkward but whatever he did we would move on and put the whole peanut butter thing behind us.

He took his bite and ate it thoughtfully, as if he were sampling a very expensive wine. I was amused by his performance. He swallowed and considered.

"That's good," he said. That was all.

I resisted apologizing. "In America kids like them."

He put his hand on mine, the way he always did when he was about to make a point he considered important. "I said it was good. Among chefs that is high praise. Flattery we leave to journalists, food critics. For a chef there are only three categories: good, acceptable, unacceptable. This sandwich you have made for me is good. With your permission I will put it on my lunch menu."

Wow. Of all the compliments I had received, this was the ultimate. Thank God it was a safe offer. No one was going to sit down in *Champ des Fraises*, open the menu, and order a peanut butter sandwich.

"I'd be honored," I said. "But I'd have to make them myself." I felt awkward. This was going to sound like boasting. "What I mean is…"

"I understand," M. Duval assured me. "The finest creations are always in the hands. A painter. Who but Monet could have painted his water lilies? Or music. A score performed by two different violinists, a master and a competent musician: the same notes but an entirely different experience. In cooking it is the same. The hands of a master are irreplaceable."

I thought of that online article about me in BuzzFeed – "The Mozart of Peanut Butter." It struck me as ridiculous at the time, but it might not have struck M. Duval the same way. And I thought of my mother's hope that one day I would become, if not a great composer, at least a great performer. Well, Mom, your dream has come true. But like all fairy tale wishes, it's a good news/bad news thing. The good news: your son is a great musician. The bad news: he plays only one piece, the Peanut Butter Sandwich in B flat.

"Your sandwiches would be on the menu for two hours each day between 11:30 and 1:30. Your responsibilities at *Champ des Fraises* would not interfere with your evenings at the club." M. Duval offered his hand. "Do we have what you Americans call a deal?"

"It would be an honor."

M. Duval introduced me to the "cold menu" kitchen at his restaurant and showed me where my station would be. I thought I could start making sandwiches right away but that is not how he did things. First we had to go to "the lab". This was a special kitchen used only to create new dishes. Believe it or not, it was a week before my peanut butter sandwiches could actually be on the menu.

According to M. Duval's professional code, you don't just pull ingredients off supermarket shelves, carry them back to the restaurant and throw them together. Everything had to be made on the premises and it had to be fresh. He set his baker to work to come up with an equivalent to Wonder bread, though what he came up with was so much better there was no comparison. Very light and airy, with a crisp, sugary crust. We decided that, given the restaurant's identifying theme, we would go with a strawberry jelly, which M. Duval concocted himself. It's a good thing he didn't put what he produced in jars and market it in stores; the world would be filled with fat people addicted to it.

The hardest thing, as I expected, was the peanut butter. M. Duval put his entire pastry staff on it but they never quite got it right. It's not that what they produced wasn't delicious. It was. In fact, they created a new tart and used it for a filling. It just wasn't American peanut butter. I explained to M. Duval that peanut butter is like a French wine. It has to come from a particular place and sit on a shelf for a while before it reaches its full potential. This made sense to him. He added that he had been worried that he was taking too much control over my "creation". "You are the magician here," he said. "Not me."

Finally, there was what M. Duval called "presentation," something I had never thought of before. Presentation is how the food looks on the plate, which is very important in a restaurant. My new and improved sandwich, made with just-baked bread, was half again as big as your normal peanut butter sandwich. When we put it on one of M. Duval's gold-rimmed plates with fresh strawberries and peach slices and a sprig of mint at the side, it looked impressive.

M. Duval put it in the dessert section of the lunch menu as *pinutte butteur surprise*. He invited a few friendly food critics to taste what he called a "special import" that had received rave reviews in the US. I was not present at that small gathering; M. Duval said it was too much to expect French food critics to be open-minded about something put together by a sixteen-year-old American.

The reviews that followed were sensational.

How did I deal with this sudden fame? No problem at all. No one knew I was the guy making the sandwiches. I did my magic – as M. Duval continued to call it – in the kitchen, out of the public eye. M. Duval did give me credit. He inserted in the lunch menu a leaflet that briefly told my story – that my sandwiches, a common mid-day meal for children, had drawn the praise of nationally known writers on food. But I remained happily hidden in the "cold menu" kitchen. In the *Champ des Fraises*, as at Rick's Café, I was invisible. And I might have stayed out of the public eye if it weren't for Marcel Bailly.

Marcel Bailly was one of the best chefs of Paris. He might have been *the* best if M. Duval hadn't already occupied that position and I guess that really grated on him. He and M. Duval were big rivals; they both had popular restaurants. M. Bailly was always looking to get an edge on M. Duval and when my peanut butter sandwich came along he found his edge. M. Bailly knew journalists who ate (cheaply) at his restaurant. They were, not surprisingly, friendly to him, ready to write an occasional puff piece when, say, a movie star or some other celebrity graced one of his tables. In this instance he asked for something more from a widely read columnist in *Paris Match*. This writer accused M. Duval of disgracing his national heritage by introducing to his menu – and publicizing! – another example of American fast food, a commonplace meal that no adult, *even in America*, would condescend to eat. This in a restaurant that, by virtue of its history and its Michelin rating, should uphold the highest culinary standards. Adding insult to injury, the "sandwich" in question (offered to patrons at the price of twelve Euros!) was made in the kitchen by an American boy in Paris on a tourist visa. If this was a joke, it was a joke in the worst taste, and a violation of French labor laws.

"It is not enough that there is a MacDonald's and a Pizza Hut on every corner. It is not enough that Coca Cola has invaded every bistro, that Mickey Mouse has built his Euro Disney Versailles on our doorstep. Now one of our premier chefs has declared publicly, yes, yes, we will serve fast food in our best restaurants. Send us more! Teach us, America, the secrets of your culinary magic!

"More than the honor of Louis Duval is at stake. At stake is the honor of France!"

I have to admit the description of my peanut butter sandwich in the piece was hilarious. But this attack on M. Duval was not funny. If a lesser chef had offered such contemptible fare it might have been laughed off. But when one of France's most distinguished chefs presented this American gruel to his guests the vulgarity could not be ignored.

"A bunny nation!" M. Duval shouted. He paced up and down as Sage translated the column for me. M. Duval pointed at the paper with a finger shaking with anger. "He say I make of France" – he could hardly get the English words out – "a bunny nation!"

"Yes," Sage said, "It's true. Here in the last sentence. 'M. Duval has committed no mere indiscretion but an abomination.'" He looked up. "He's crazy. No one will take him seriously."

"Of course he is crazy," M. Duval exclaimed. "That is why he will be taken seriously."

He knew the columnist's association with M. Bailly and realized immediately the source of his troubles. He knew that other journalists who were friends of M. Bailly would take up the attack. There would be letters to the editors of all the important (and not so important) papers. What he did not foresee was that *The New York Times* Paris Bureau would send someone with a photographer to capitalize on this opportunity. There I was in the digital edition under the headline "A Revolution in French Cuisine?" wearing an apron and a chef's cap. Not even M. Bailly could have imagined a better way to splash the flames of controversy with gasoline: Paris Is Burning!

I was now definitely in the public eye. Who was this Rick Hasselbach and what was his relationship with Louis Duval? One resourceful journalist turned up at Rick's Café and by questioning the staff learned of M. Duval's involvement with it. Fortunately, my invisibility at the club had an unforeseen benefit. No one on the staff could say for sure what my role there was – if I had a role. The reporter showed them the photographs in the digital *New York Times* story and they said things like, "Oh, the boy in the white dinner jacket?" and shrugged. But in the article he wrote, the reporter made much of M. Duval: Why in the world was a chef of his standing operating a rock club with an American theme pitched to a young clientele? He had leased the premises only for the summer. It made no fiscal sense; it made no sense at all. The reporter had made another puzzling discovery as well. Young Hasselbach was living in Louis Duval's *maison*.

M. Duval had his supporters, of course. But they too were baffled by Rick's Café. And why did he have a child on the staff, featured in the menu of his three-star restaurant and ensconced in his domicile? No one seemed to know what to make of the elderly icon. Had he gone round the bend? M. Duval maintained a steadfast silence in public. Social media was not silent, however. I was fast becoming a "fake news" meme.

At that point he and I were invited to appear together on a popular talk show on French television to tell our side of the story. The host, Marc Halle, had the reputation of being a fair but tough questioner. Normally he did not interrogate his guests but there had been occasions when he had. Was his invitation an opportunity or a trap?

CHAPTER 9

M. Duval, Sage, Danielle and I sat around the table in M. Duval's kitchen. Sal was off with Dirty Laundry. I didn't see a whole lot of Sal these days. I guess you could say our careers were taking us in different directions. Anyway, we were debating whether or not M. Duval and I should agree to be on the talk show. M. Duval had been on television before, though on programs dealing with food, situations in which he was entirely comfortable. He didn't like the idea of having to defend himself against ridiculous allegations. Appearing to take them seriously, he would only enhance their credibility. He had reservations about a talk show format; he was unfamiliar with Marc Halle and his show, having never seen it. Most nights he was at the *Champ des Fraises*. Was it really necessary for him to join this media circus?

Yes, said Sage, arguing the other side. The media was already parading M. Duval under the big top. The allegations and the misleading inferences from limited information *had* raised legitimate questions for M. Duval's friends and supporters. From the outside, M. Duval's connection with my café and my responsibilities at *Champ des Fraises* were hard to understand. Sage had gone on the Internet to make a Google search into this talk show and found that it was a respected venue that often explored important issues. Political figures and academics had been guests. Given the publicity surrounding the controversy in the wake of the *Times* story, M. Duval would have the widest audience to put everything in the proper perspective.

M. Duval, however, was not the only one who had been invited. There was me. I had already made a fool of myself at the café trying to make like Humphrey Bogart; I didn't want to make a fool of myself on French television. And I certainly didn't want to get M. Duval into more trouble. There was my very imperfect French, which would only become more garbled under studio lights in front of a live audience.

Sage played the devil's advocate, not arguing for or against but asking the tough questions. He began by conceding my point about language. "If this interview were going to be conducted in English, I'd say go for it. In French I'm not so sure."

"Why?" Danielle asked.

"He could choke. Hot lights, a live telecast. I'd choke and my French is better than Rick's."

"You're too modest." Danielle just didn't like the guy.

"This is time for straight talk," Sage shot back. "It won't help Rick to push him into a situation he can't handle." He turned to me. "You know what I'm saying?"

"Sure," I said. Sage's frankness didn't bother me. That's what I needed – reality testing. "I agree with you. I don't think my French is good enough to go on a show like that."

"Have you seen this show?" Sage asked Danielle.

"I've seen it," she said. "I'm not a regular viewer."

"What's Marc Halle like? Aggressive or friendly?"

"Both. He can go from friendly to aggressive in a heartbeat. He wants to probe. It's what makes his show interesting."

"Where does he stand on France for the French?" Sage pressed.

"I don't know," Danielle admitted.

"And we don't have time to find out." Sage shook his head. "We have to give him an answer in twenty-four hours." He considered for a moment, then turned to Danielle. "Do you think this guy would be willing to conduct the interview in English?" Our entire conversation so far had been in English, in deference to me.

"No he won't," Danielle said. "His audience is French-speaking. And it wouldn't be a good idea from our point of view. If Rick can't speak French at all, it won't matter what he says, he'll make a bad impression. Halting French is better than no French at all."

"What if I say I don't want to go on," I said.

Again, Sage was the devil's advocate. "That has its downside too. It will look like you're afraid to answer some of the questions that might come up. Or they might decide to pair M. Duval with someone hostile to our side."

"You're a very encouraging person," Danielle said. "It's so important to have a friend that believes in you."

Sage let that pass. He wasn't going to get into an argument.

"Now, now," M. Duval said. "Sage is doing a good thing. He is making us think clearly. At this moment we need to think clearly."

"I'm going on the show," I said. My voice sounded like I knew what I was doing, which was news to me.

"You're sure that's what you want?" Sage asked.

"I'm sure. When will we be interviewed?"

"Next week," said Sage. "This controversy is hot right now but they don't know how long it will stay hot." He turned to me. "You think you can be ready in a week?"

"As ready as I'll ever be," I said, "If you and Danielle will coach me."

"How can I help?" Sage asked.

"Danielle is a terrific language teacher but you can ask me the tough questions they might throw at me. We'll rehearse and rehearse, the way they do with candidates before a political debate."

"Do you think you can do it?" Danielle asked.

"I've got to," I said. I had remembered that saying of Emerson's Aunt Moody: Always do what you are afraid to do. She better be right, I thought.

I better be right.

CHAPTER 10

I think the word for it is sequester. In my English dictionary sequester means "to remove or set apart, to withdraw, into seclusion." The French word is *séquestrer*. That's the kind of French word I like; the kind that is almost the same as the English except for the extra r or e. Of course, there's that pronunciation thing. *Séquestrer*. "The r comes farther back, Rick. Listen. *Séquestrer*." For one week I was sequestered with Danielle and Sage. For one week I lived, breathed, and ate French. For one week I was grilled as if I were auditioning for the voice of the French people. No, no, Rick. *Séquestrer*. Listen to the r. *Séquestrer*.

One good thing about the ordeal: Danielle began to give Sage a little credit. The guy is one hell of a teacher and after awhile even she could see that. She was too. I couldn't have asked for better coaches, even if I were preparing for the Olympics, which I was. Don't worry, I won't give you the blow-by-blow. I had to go through it, but there is no reason you have to.

So. The magic hour rolls around. Showtime. Danielle, Sage, and I are driven to the studio by a chauffer from the television station. M. Duval will come to the studio directly from the *Champ des Fraises*. "I still have a business to run," was his final comment to us. We're going to see if Danielle can go on with me as a backup translator. I won't use her unless I absolutely have to. For instance, if I have to say something especially complicated or I have to be really diplomatic. Probably I won't need her at all, but if I do, she's there – assuming she is allowed to participate.

I'm taken to the makeup room where they spent thirty minutes getting me ready. Then I'm introduced to Marc Halle, who seems like a friendly enough guy, though I have no idea how sincere he is. While we're talking a woman comes up and takes him aside for a private chat. What she tells him puts a stricken look on his face. Suddenly there is a bad vibe and people are rushing around in a panicky way. Something has come up. Marc Halle returns to me and says, "We have just learned that Louis Duval has been taken to the hospital."

Now I'm the one with the stricken face. "What?"

"He may have had a heart attack."

I'm feeling sick and dizzy.

"We need to make a decision," M. Halle says. "Do we go on without him?" I must look stunned because he quickly adds, "Of course, it will be our decision, but I need to know if you would be willing to go on alone." He glances at his watch. "We'll need to decide in the next few minutes."

I'm breathing heavily. I can't think, so I don't know where my answer comes from. "I'll go on."

He nods and goes off to confer with whoever. He comes back. "It's a go." We walk together to two chairs on the dais. I sit down, he sits down. There is no chair for Danielle. There is no Danielle. Just bright lights and cameras and a lot of faces staring at me. M.Halle says something to the audience about M. Duval not being present and for the next half hour my mind is a total blank. I mean, nothing registers. Then I'm aware of walking from the set. People are clapping. Back stage, Sage pumps my hand. "Great interview!" he says, "You were fantastic." I'm in a state of shock. "Take me to M. Duval," I say.

We're in a hospital, a waiting room. Aunt Polly Esther and Sal have been there for some time, but haven't been informed of M. Duval's status. Finally a doctor comes and tells us that M. Duval has had an "event" of some kind. He is okay; it's not critical but he is being kept in the hospital overnight. He will be operated on the next day and a "stent" will be placed in an artery, a common operation with almost no risk. He is asleep so we can't talk with him. We should go home. We shouldn't worry.

We go home and I go to bed but I do not sleep.

This is the worst night of my life.

On the afternoon of the next day we are finally able to see M. Duval. In his bed he looks tired but not like he's at death's door. "You really didn't want to do that interview, did you?" Sage jokes.

M. Duval grins and raises his hand. "Please, don't make me laugh." He looks at me. "The nurses tell me you were wonderful."

"They saw the show?" Danielle says with surprise.

"It seems everyone saw the show but me."

"M. Duval," I said. "I'm so sorry."

"Sorry? You were a hit."

"If it weren't for me, none of this would have happened."

"Rick, I was the one who insisted you make your sandwiches at the *Champ des Fraises*. It serves me right for exploiting unpaid, undocumented labor." We couldn't laugh but we did grin. The old M. Duval was on the road to recovery.

"Okay, let's see what all the excitement is about."

Danielle had brought her laptop and opened it to the Marc Halle show on YouTube.

It was a very strange, out-of-body experience for me. I had no recollection of any of this so I viewed the proceedings with a weird detachment. At first the "me" on the screen had a kind of deer-caught-in-the-headlights look on his face. Marc Halle spent the first minutes asking me simple questions, putting me at ease, and I did seem to become calmer. Then he gradually led me into the controversy. I have to say he was a very skillful questioner. He wasn't out to nail me; he wanted to find out what was going on. I must have picked up on that because soon I was answering his questions straightforwardly.

M. Halle took up the matter of peanut butter sandwiches on the menu of a premier restaurant and my fame as a maker of such. Sage had prepped me for this inevitable challenge. The dreaded hamburger – the most notorious of American fast foods – had recently been transformed by three-star Paris chefs, I said. I named names: Stephen d'Aboville, Nicholas Castellet. Yorrick Alleno had a Michelin three-star chuck-and-beef-rib smoked beef bacon cheeseburger on the menu (for 30 euros!) at the lunchroom of the swank Hotel Le Meurice. "Marcel Bailly has also embraced the hamburger," I said. "His version uses truffles and foie gras. I've heard it is quite tasty." I added that M. Duval had not himself taken up this new food fashion.

My reference to M. Duval gave M. Halle his opportunity to segue into my puzzling relationship with Paris's renowned chef. I began with my visit to Mr. Peppercorn – I didn't think to call him Ainsworth Fogdingle – where he told me of his friendship with M. Duval. I told of how Mr. Peppercorn came upon M. Duval cooking an omelet in a bombed out restaurant after the Allies had entered Paris; how M. Duval had fought in the Resistance, living at times on roots and grasses, dreaming of the day he would return to Paris and make that omelet; how Mr. Peppercorn used his army connections to get food for the Duval family and became part of the family. I said that Mr. Peppercorn had sent Sage and Sal and Aunt Polly Esther and me to Paris because I had told him of my Casablanca fantasy. M. Duval had welcomed us and helped us in so many ways. He even graciously hosted a family picnic at his vacation home on the Fourth of July.

That was the gist of my story and I have to say it *is* a terrific story of French-American friendship. All I did was tell it in my halting French, but I could see that my limited language skills had an advantage. I came across as completely sincere. I wasn't trying to make an impression or score points. I was obviously struggling to do my best at the most basic level. I could see how I might even seem, at moments, touching to a French audience. It was clear how much I respected M. Duval and how generous he had been to young people he had not known before that summer. What had started out as a favor to an old friend had become much more than that.

Near the end Marc Halle said, "I believe Americans have an expression, 'No good deed goes unpunished.'" He said it in English and translated it into French. "That seems to be the case here." Then he drew the interview to a close. "You have experienced more of Paris than any tourist during your short time here," he said. "What is the most vivid memory you will take back with you?"

I didn't answer right away. All I could think of was Danielle showing me Paris.

"Learning to speak French," I said.

The audience exploded with applause and I was led from the dais.

The television screen went blank. M. Duval looked over to me and said, "You done good, kid." I realized his American English was better than my French.

As we were leaving the hospital, Sal congratulated me. She hadn't been able to see the interview the night before because she had been anxiously awaiting word about M. Duval in the hospital waiting room. "You came across really well," she said, then added, "Will you be at the club tonight?"

I suddenly realized that it had been a while since I had made an appearance. Preparing for the interview had absorbed me 24/7.

"I'm not sure," I said. "I didn't get any sleep last night. I might crash early this evening."

"At least put in a few hours," she said. "I think Dirty Laundry has gotten a lot better." She smiled at me. "I've even developed some style." So of course I promised I'd be there. It had been a while since I had seen Sal perform. But I have to say, by this point Rick's Café had come to feel like it was more trouble than it was worth.

I went home and collapsed in bed. At 6:00 Sage banged on my door and woke me up. I grabbed a bite and raced off to the club. There was a line as usual so I ducked in through a back door and got into my dinner jacket and tie. The waiters came up and congratulated me on my interview. I felt for the first time that it registered on them who I was.

The doors opened and that's when I learned that I had, overnight, become a celebrity. "Hey, Rick!" "Good job, Rick!" "Rick!" My circulating problems, it seemed, were a thing of the past.

CHAPTER 11

M. Duval spent a couple days in the hospital and then he came home. He seemed as fit as ever, but his doctor had cautioned against returning to business as usual, certainly in the short term. In the long term, he urged, M. Duval should consider turning over some of his responsibilities at the restaurant to his staff. Now that I was working in one of the kitchens, I could see the relentless stress that comes with running a place like that. The doctor carefully avoided the dreaded word retirement but M. Duval was unusually quiet at home; I think he was weighing his options.

He was right about success, by the way. It's important to celebrate it before it comes because afterward you're too busy to enjoy it. The next weeks rushed by. *Pinutte butteur surprises* were the hot item at the *Champ des Fraises* now. Two very aggressive guys showed up and presented me with a business proposition, a franchise – Peanut Butter Paradise. At the caf*e* I discovered that when you move around in a crowd chatting with strangers all night, it gives you a headache. I understood why Bogart's Rick never sat down with his customers. It was too late for me to adopt that policy. I had already established my Joe Friendly personality and I could hardly shift into reverse without coming across as a conceited jerk. The problem is, when you meet a lot of people you don't get connected to anyone in particular. There were girls who indicated in one way or another that they were available for a connection but, like Bogart, I was interested in only one woman and I was seeing less and less of her.

Sal and Dirty Laundry played in the club most nights. She had by now developed a style that spliced punk and innocence in a way that was, I have to admit, seductive. She projected a double message: I'm a good girl, but I get crazy at times. Wanna get crazy? Looking around at the crowd, I saw that more than one guy wouldn't mind taking her up on that. I began to wonder what sort of off-stage life she was leading. I hoped the Jeans were looking after her. She was, after all, still a minor.

Danielle was off with Aunt Poly Esther. Remember Aunt Polly Esther? I haven't said much about her because for most of the summer she had been doing her own thing. I'd assumed that meant research for her diet book. You know, France on 1,500 calories a day? Not so. It seems that Aunt Polly Esther had taken offence at Paris fashions, at least the kind you see on magazine covers. She felt that these clothes were silly and cumbersome to wear and that the skinny models who wore them bore no resemblance to actual human beings. This has been said many times before, but the difference between Aunt Polly Esther and your ordinary person is that when Aunt Polly Esther feels strongly about something she doesn't just talk.

She had decided that Paris needed a new fashion designer with a new approach to women's clothing. "Real clothes for real women" is how Aunt Polly Esther put it. She made Sage her "creative consultant"; he had a long history of standing conventional wisdom on its head. Their first challenge, she told him, was to reinvent the common housecoat worn by stay-at-home wives, a housecoat that would change their self-image and get them out of the home. Not only that, Aunt Polly Esther wanted her garments to be modeled by middle-aged women. That's right. Reubens-size fannies wagging up and down the world's most famous runway.

When she confided her concept to M. Duval, he nodded reflectively, as he had when she first told him she would write a book about traveling in France on 1,500 calories a day. M. Duval had made his adjustment to Aunt Polly Esther. He told her she would have to go before a panel of jurors to get permission to exhibit her housecoats, though he cautioned that even getting an audience before the jurors would be a long shot. Ever the diplomat, he avoided the word impossible, though he did suggest that fashion shows, unlike flea markets, were not open to all vendors.

Aunt Polly Esther, however, was not a woman to walk away from a closed door. A woman who attempts every form of fiction before inventing an entirely new one does not give up easily. She set to work. I had plenty going on in my life so I'm vague on the details but she and Sage began to sketch and mock up housecoats. They had a few parameters: Bold colors, big pockets, bright lining. Something like that. As I say, I wasn't paying much attention – until they were joined by Danielle. Because Sage's time away from the project to coach me for the Marc Halle Show put them behind schedule, Danielle volunteered to help out. She had had a funky knack of reinventing herself in my French lessons in Paris, with her Dadaist, don't-be-afraid-to-be-ridiculous approach to style, but I'm not sure just what she was contributing. All I know is that I was seeing very little of her.

The second week of August she and Sage asked if they could use my cafe one afternoon to show some of their housecoats to a couple of the Paris fashion show jurors. It seems M. Duval had pulled some strings with these guys who were regulars at the *Champ des Fraises*. They wouldn't be seeing "Polly Esther Potter's Real Clothes for Real Women" by the way. M. Duval told them her name would doom the project, as would the concept. The jurors would be shown Casual Wear by Sagittarius. In an ironic twist of fate, the name Sagittarius would open rather than close doors.

I said, sure, they could use the club. The forties look would be a cool retro setting for a style that was itself retro. I didn't go to the viewing; I was working at the *Champ des Fraises* at the time. Afterward Sage and Danielle said they thought it went well. I was glad to see how well they got along. I had always thought they had a lot in common. The jurors told them they would notify them in a week on

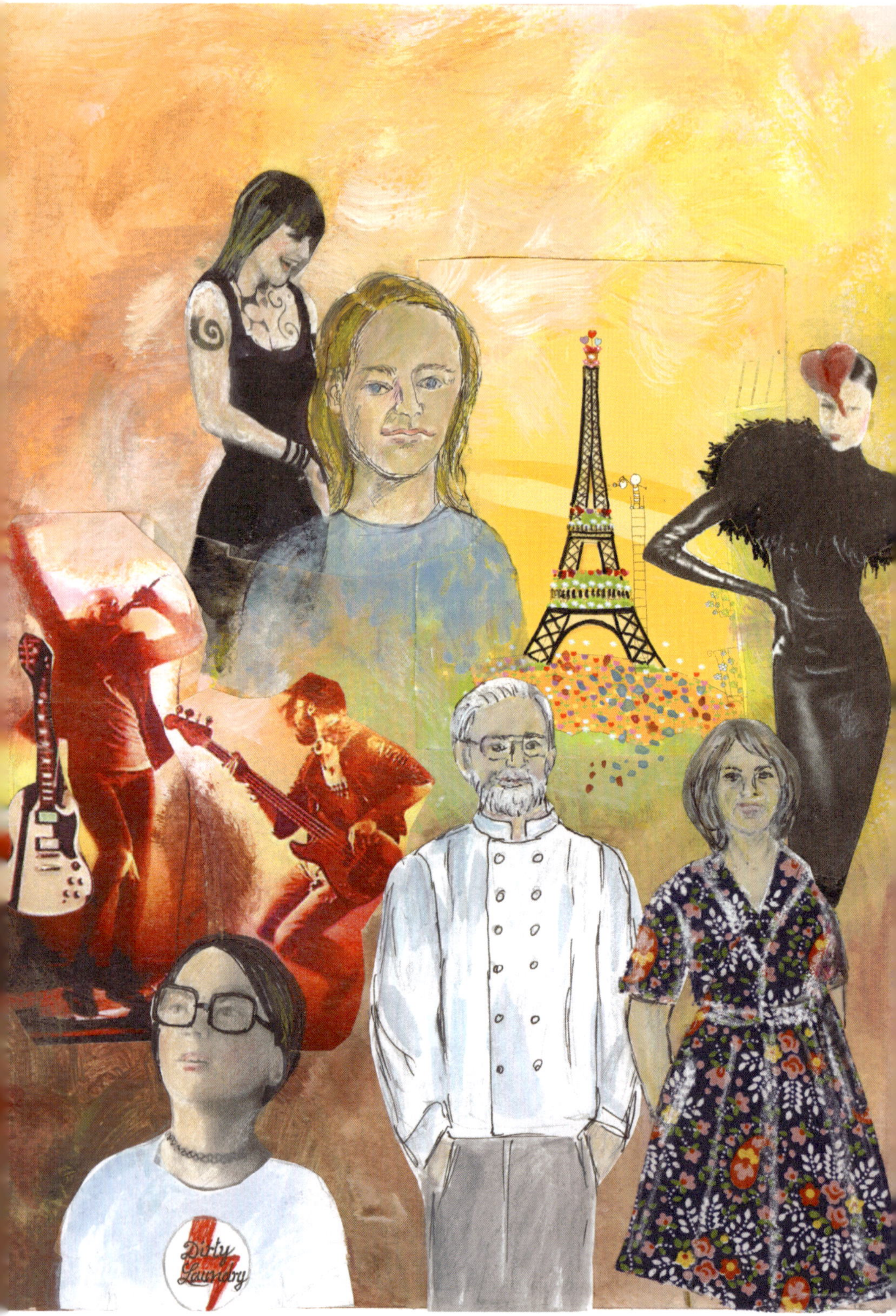
Dirty Laundry

their decision.

"What if they give you the go-ahead?" I asked Aunt Polly Esther.

"I'd have to extend my stay in Paris," she said.

"Sage too?"

"Oh yes. I'd need Sage here with me. It'll be just a few extra months."

"Hmm. What if they turn you down?"

"I have a Plan B. I'll find another venue and rent it during the spring fashion show."

"That could be expensive."

"Not a problem, I've got the money. This is a real opportunity, not just for me but for women everywhere."

CHAPTER 12

At supper Sage and Danielle were too excited to eat. There had been a new development in the "What does it mean to be French?" debate. Marine Le Pen, a right-wing leader of the *Front National* party had, for obscure reasons, decided to turn her attention to M. Duval. Usually her thing was keeping out North African immigrants, people that, she claimed, stole jobs from "real" Frenchmen. Her party represented only a fraction of the parliament. Normally you wouldn't expect her to have an opinion – at least in public – on haute cuisine or popular music.

She had just made a speech to some of her followers in the Faubourg Saint-Antoine, the site of past revolutions. She had used M. Duval as an example of what she called "the new Trojan horse," the invasion of the French economy by American entrepreneurs. Hot dogs, Coca Cola, rock and peanut butter got lumped together.

"Take this Rick's Café that we have heard so much about recently, a club modeled on a Hollywood movie. We're told it is no more than a boy's dream, the dream of Rick Hasselbach. Does anyone believe that a boy is the intelligence behind the *Café Américain*? Do they imagine we are dupes? No, the club, that has been launched with unprecedented publicity, is the flagship of a franchise that will soon replicate itself like a poison mushroom throughout the city of Paris and France itself. Our young people will soon be flocking – even as they are doing today – to this new temple of American pop culture."

Danielle refused to take the speech seriously. "Le Pen is a demagogue. Who listens to her? Only little people afraid of the future, afraid they will lose their jobs if outsiders are allowed to come to France. Except among a few, she is not respected."

"Ten percent is more than a few," said Sage.

"It will never be a majority," Danielle retorted. "It will disperse like a crowd."

I would have hung around to hear more but I had to get to the club. I was already an hour late. Dirty Laundry would be playing that night.

It was 8:30 when I got there, an hour before the place would fill. A warm-up band was playing. Sal came over and sat down.

"Hello, stranger," I said.

"You're the stranger. I never see you anymore."

"It's been a crazy time, getting ready for the interview with Marc Halle."

"Must be hard being a celebrity."

"Harder than you'd think."

"You've sure picked up a lot of French."

"That's Danielle. She coached me for a solid week."

"Danielle seems to be your all-round handler. I'm surprised she isn't at your side now."

"Don't be catty. She's helping Aunt Polly Esther and Sage put together their fashion line." I looked at her. "Your hair is different. The short cut brings out your eyes. It goes well with your new performance style"

"I got it cut two weeks ago. Finally you noticed."

"I noticed before this.

"Then why didn't you tell me? You haven't said anything about my 'new performance style.'"

I shrugged. "It's like I said, things have been crazy lately. Anyway, I like your new look."

She smiled. "Thanks." Sometimes it's so easy to please Sal. "Jean-Luc and Jean-Michel helped me with it."

"How are the Jeans, by the way?"

"They're fine. They've been very good friends to me."

"There's something else."

"What?"

"About you. There's something else."

"I cleaned my teeth."

I studied her more closely. "You're wearing different glasses."

"Do you like them?"

I nodded approval. "Definitely. The black frames with your hair cut short makes you look more sophisticated."

"I *am* more sophisticated," she said and got up and left.

It got to be nine o'clock and Dirty Laundry came on. We had a full house, though there was something different about the crowd. We seemed to be attracting a more diverse clientele.

Dirty Laundry's opening set was pretty familiar by now and I tuned out. There was only a week and a half left of our time in Paris. It was hard to imagine life back in the States after all that had happened. It was especially hard to imagine leaving Danielle. I started thinking of how I could express my gratitude for all she had done for me. If only there were some way…and then it hit me. Of course! A plane ticket to America. The perfect gift. She'd never been to America. It would have to be an open ticket, where she could pick her departure and return dates. There had to be some way to arrange that.

When she came I'd show her Chicago, with its awesome skyline. I'd take her to the top of the Sears Tower for a view of the city lit up at night. I'd give her a tour of the town, the way she'd shown me Paris. There would be some high culture stuff, the Institute of Art, the Symphony (Mom would get us box seats). I'd tell her about the Second City Theater and how it gave all those Saturday Night Live greats their first big break. Those classic French themes of love and politics? President Obama started his political career in Chicago; he met and fell in love with Michelle there. (They still had their home in the city. Where? Find out.)

When it got time for Danielle to return to France I'd notice that she was getting moody. The night before her departure, we'd go for a walk. A long, sad walk, maybe along Lake Michigan. We would stop and look out across the water – it would be dusk – and Danielle would break down. "I can't do it, Rick," she'd say, choking on her tears. "The day you left Paris, if you knew what I went through... Now...I know I'll never have the strength to leave you again...I can't fight it anymore...I wish I didn't love you so much."

Something in the club pulled me back into reality. All around guys were standing up. Dirty Laundry had come back from their break and Sal was stepping up to the mic.

Just then these guys scattered around the room started singing *La Marseillaise,* the French national anthem. It's famous; you've probably heard it. I like it. But I didn't know what they were doing singing it in the *Café Américain.* I didn't recognize any of them as regular customers. They weren't in a group, close together, but here and there around the room. At first I didn't know what to make of it and then I realized they meant to cause a disturbance.

I knew enough French to understand some of the words of *La Marseillaise.* I don't know if you know what those words are but some of the lyrics are violent. The song came out of the French Revolution. "Do you hear in our countryside/ The roaring of ferocious soldiers/ They are walking right into our arms/ Form your battalions/ Let us march, let us march, till their impure blood waters our furrows." These guys leaned into the violent parts, sang them loud and very clearly. Their faces dared you to try to stop them.

I felt very self-conscious. This was Rick's Café and I was Rick. I was the guy in the white dinner jacket. What was I going to do? Take on all these guys, any one of whom could beat me to a pulp? We didn't have any bouncers in the club; we'd never needed any before. I felt people starting to look at me, watching to see what I would do. I was hot and flushed and clueless.

Out of the void I heard this voice. It was Sal singing into the mic: "Hey, Jude." It took a minute for the Jeans to realize what she was doing but then they gave her backup. She stood there singing, one voice against their voices. She seemed very calm. *La Marseillaise* got louder and louder until you could barely hear her. But she kept singing. "Hey, Jude, don't make it bad, take a sad song and make it better."

Then, one by one, others in the club stood up and started singing "Hey, Jude." Within a minute everyone was standing and singing. Now it was *La Marseillaise* you could barely hear. It was a standoff but it didn't look like these guys would go without a fight.

BANG! The front door was slammed open and half a dozen guys in black ski masks barged in wielding baseball bats. (I thought they were baseball bats. Do they have baseball bats in France? I'm not sure they play baseball.) Whatever they were wielding, they were doing major damage to the bar and everything behind it. They didn't go after people, just inventory. Their rampage seemed to go on forever, but it probably didn't last more than five minutes. As suddenly as they came, they were gone.

We stood around in stunned silence and then a guy pointed to one of the *Marseillaise* singers and shouted, "He called them. I heard him. He called them on his cell phone!" At that point fists started flying, a rock 'em, sock 'em mêlée that spilled out of doors. It couldn't have been more than a couple of minutes before the street was filled with sirens, police cars, gendarmes, and shortly thereafter television vans with reporters and cameramen.

In my brief time in France I had experienced fancy meals, the Mona Lisa, cheek kissing, the Eiffel Tower lit up at night – the usual tourist stuff. But they had saved something special just for me because I wasn't your ordinary tourist. To me they gave this last gift wrapped in tissue paper with a bow – a traditional Paris riot. They loved me that much.

CHAPTER 13

As we walked through the rubble the next morning I felt bad for M. Duval. How could he have known when he showed us kindness that he would be paid back with so much grief, but he was cool about it. "Freedom cost me a lot more sixty years ago," he said. "This is nothing." When I'm in my seventies, I want to have his attitude. Fortunately he was covered by insurance. But the money wasn't the issue with him. When we went for lunch, he handed me a check for a thousand euros.

"What is this for?" I asked.

"For your work at the *Champ des Fraises*," he said.

"I can't accept this," I said, "Not after what happened at the club. Besides, I made my sandwiches at the restaurant for the honor of it. What a privilege – and a learning experience."

"I know you didn't do it for money," he said, "But you've worked very hard in my kitchen for weeks. This payment is a point of honor for me. I will be extremely unhappy if you refuse to accept what are your rightful wages." His face made it clear he was serious about this.

What could I do? I accepted the check, but there was no way I was going to spend this money on myself.

Sage, Danielle, Sal and I and the staff at the club spent the rest of the day sweeping up and trying to create some semblance of order in the premises. Most of the tables and chairs, though nicked and scuffed, were still usable. The bar was gashed in places but still recognizably a bar. The shelves behind it were completely trashed and all the bottles broken. The coffee maker functioned. About six o'clock we were getting ready to leave when Sal said, "Take a look outside." Sage and I followed her to the door and opened it: a line stretched down the block. We asked the kids at the front of the line what they were waiting for and they said they were waiting for the club to open. We told them the club had been trashed the night before and they said they knew that. We said we had nothing to serve inside; no bands would be playing.

By now a small crowd was gathered around the entrance. We've brought our own stuff, some of them said, and lifted up coolers and back packs. Some had brought guitars. "You aren't going to let a bunch of goons close down the club are you?" one guy asked. "Can you give us a moment?" Sage said and we retreated inside to figure out what to do.

"Let's bring them in," Sage said. "Obviously they came to make a statement and I think it's a statement that ought to be made."

None of us could argue with that so we opened the doors and the folks outside filed in. In fact, they filed in throughout the evening, and not just our usual crowd. There were working people and white-collar types, older people who might have been grandparents. Pretty much every demographic was represented. I suppose you could call it a non-violent protest of the violence of the night before. Coolers and backpacks were opened and soft drinks and bottles of wine and paper cups were passed around. Those with guitars played them, though nobody took to the stage. The whole thing really moved me; the vibe was so amazing. People stood around or sat and smoked and talked. When the last of them left at around midnight we discovered that someone had left a guitar case. It was filled with euros. Throughout the week money would come by mail as well, more than a thousand euros in all. A bittersweet ending to the cafe

As we closed up, I went to Sal and said, "Sal, I wanted to tell you that you were terrific yesterday. That took real guts."

She shrugged in that aw shucks way she has.

"You've come so far in such a short time."

"It took me a while to find it. My style."

There was a pause and then she said, "We're having a little party at Jean-Michel's tomorrow night. You're one of the guests of honor.

We can talk more then."

I wanted to have dinner with Danielle that evening and give her the plane ticket. "Gee, Sal, that's…thanks, I'd love to. But I have a commitment."

All the light went out of her face.

"Hey, in a few days we'll have nothing but time together. I suspect we'll spend all next year talking about this summer."

She didn't say anything.

"Tell you what. I'll try to get away early from this thing I'm tied up with. I may be able to make it. How late will your party be going?"

"I don't know. It depends."

"I'll try to get there."

Outside the club I saw Sage and Danielle together; she was in the middle of a laughing fit. "I've got to run," Sage said as I came up and left.

'What's so funny?" I asked Danielle.

"Oh nothing. I think it's exhaustion. I haven't been getting much sleep." She looked at her watch. "I should go home."

"I was wondering if we might have dinner together tomorrow evening."

She didn't answer right away and I sensed she was running something through her mind. "Thanks, that would be nice. Could we make it early? I have a commitment later in the evening."

I was bit disappointed; I didn't want to share her tomorrow evening with anyone else. But what could I do? My invitation was on short notice.

"How about seven o'clock?" I named a bistro, one of the few eating places I was familiar with that was fairly inexpensive.

"Seven it is." She leaned forward and kissed me on my cheek. "This has been a wonderful night. One of the most wonderful nights of my life."

I watched her walk away. Hey, Jude, don't let me down. You have found her, now go and get her.

CHAPTER 14

I spent the next day setting up my surprise for Danielle that evening – a plane ticket to America. At first I thought I wouldn't be able to swing it. I considered borrowing from Aunt Polly Esther but she might have to shell out a lot of euros for this exhibit she was putting together. And anyway, she would want to keep Danielle in Paris to look after her fashion line until the spring show. I didn't want to have to wait that long to bring Danielle to the States.

Then I remembered the thousand euro check M. Duval had given me. I didn't want to spend it on myself but if I used it to pay for Danielle's airfare I wouldn't be spending it on myself. I ran my idea past M. Duval to see what he thought. He nodded reflectively.

"Danielle will be involved with her studies until December," he said.

"It would be an open ticket," I reminded him. "She could choose her departure date."

"And if she declines your offer," he said, "Would you be able to get a refund?"

"Why would she turn down a flight to the States?"

He smiled. "Why indeed? Certainly. Clearly this is something you want very much, so why not? She will be moved by your generosity."

"Will you go with me to a travel agent and help me buy it?"

"Yes I will."

So we went to a travel agent he had often used and the transaction went surprisingly quickly. The agent even got me a good price as a favor to M. Duval. When we left I was walking on air.

Our dinner at the bistro that evening couldn't have gone better. Danielle and I looked back on the summer and all the crazy things that had happened. "This summer has changed my life," I told her. "It has changed mine as well," she said. My heart pounded so hard I was afraid she might hear it. At the end I handed an envelope with the airline ticket to her.

"What is this?" she said and started to open it.

"No, no, don't open it here. Wait till you get home. It's a surprise."

"Rick, I hope this isn't money."

"It isn't," I assured her. "It's something much better than money."

"Well thank you."

After we parted I checked my watch. There was still plenty of time to join the celebration at the Jeans' studio, but I just wasn't in the mood for a party without Danielle. I went back to M. Duval's and tucked in early. I hadn't been getting much sleep lately.

Two days later I got a letter in the mail. Inside was the airline ticket and a note. "Dear Rick, Your invitation and gift are wonderful but I cannot accept them. There are things we must talk about. Can we meet soon? Your friend, Danielle."

There are things we must talk about. Your friend, Danielle. That was the killer. Your friend.

I spent the day walking, as if this feeling in my gut was a cramp and I might walk it off. I went back to all the places that Danielle had taken me to during those first weeks. It was like watching a movie I had seen before. No, not watching. Reliving a movie that was my life, like the long flashback where Rick remembers all the wonderful times in Paris when he first got to know Ilsa. I went to the Faubourg Saint-Antoine and the Bastille. She had shown up that day wearing trousers and a man's shirt and tie and a man's felt hat. "Today I am George Sand." She smoked cigars as she told me about the Paris of Revolution. "I am a Romantic. I am for all people." I could see that huge painting, "Liberty Leading the People," as clearly as if I were standing before it.

I went to the financial district where Danielle, with her eye patch and her chocolate moustache, danced her stupid Dadaist dance around the guys in suits. "If you are afraid of being ridiculous you will never be free." I went to the café where Hemingway wrote *The Sun Also Rises*. I went to Pére Lachaise and stood at the tomb of Eloise and Abelard, their sad ending. "No, not sad. Bittersweet. Bittersweet endings have more emotions."

I walked and walked and walked. In the afternoon the sky darkened and it started to pour, as if the director of the movie-that-is-my-life had called out, "Cue the weather!" I didn't have an umbrella but it didn't matter. The looks people gave me didn't matter. I had to drag myself through every miserable memory. Around 4:00 I was so exhausted I couldn't take another step. I decided to take the Métro back.

Down on the platform there was just me and an old fellow in a cloth cap and a shabby coat sitting on a bench. Was he waiting for a train or was he a homeless person who had come down here to get out of the rain? I sort of connected with his downtrodden spirit. I thought of that game Sage had invented on our plane flight to Paris, the round-robin storytelling about a memory peddler who went through a village trading memories. The old guy on the bench looked like he could have been that peddler.

The game had seemed far-fetched to me when Sage proposed it, but now I wasn't so sure. If I had the chance to unload all my painful memories of Danielle, would I take it? At that moment it sure was tempting. I remembered one of the stories Sal told in the round-robin game. An old woman gave the peddler a memory of a country-dance where she had fallen in love with a young man in the village. When she was young, she had worked the counter in a bakery in town and this guy often dropped by in the afternoon to buy something sweet, so she saw him a lot. She thought he was handsome and she sometimes fantasized about how they might get to know each other better.

She daydreamed about him during the slow hours at the bakery.

When there was the dance in the village she didn't usually go because she was shy but she did go this one time and somehow found herself dancing with the boy of her daydreams. I think Sal had said he had just broken up with his regular girlfriend. Anyway, this guy stayed with her throughout the dance and walked her home and kissed her goodnight. That was all. The next week he came to the bakery and bought something but gave no indication that anything was different between them. Later she learned that he was back with his girlfriend; in a couple of years they would get married. But the girl in the bakery would never marry.

As she grew older she never forgot the night she fell in love with the boy at the dance. The memory was always brand-new, as if she had polished it on a regular basis. If it was so important to her, why did she give it to the memory peddler after all those years, I asked Sal. Sal shrugged and said, It's Aunt Polly Esther's turn, and handed the story off to her. The old woman was doing some sensible housecleaning, was the way Aunt Polly Esther ended the story.

I thought about my memories of Danielle. Would I have them with me for the rest of my life? Would they keep me from falling in love with someone else, at least falling as intensely as I had for her? If that old guy sitting on the bench suddenly got up and walked over to me and said, Got any memories you don't need, what would I say to him? My memory of Danielle wasn't one special night, but a lot of big and small memories. If I wanted to erase them I'd have to erase most of my summer. There is no way I would do that.

So how long would I be carrying around this misery? Months? Years?

When I got back to M. Duval's, Sage was sitting at the kitchen table. I dropped into a chair across from him, more tired than I had ever been in my life. Neither of us said anything. Then Sage cleared his throat.

"Danielle told me about the airplane ticket."

"Yeah. That was pretty stupid."

"It wasn't stupid. Maybe a little reckless."

"Always do what you are afraid to do."

"So you understood the risk."

"No I didn't. I didn't know what I was doing. I was in love." Am in love.

"She's older than you are."

I nodded.

"Did you consider that she might be in love with someone else?"

"No. I suppose I didn't want to entertain that possibility. She was in love with someone once, an American, but that was years ago."

"I know," he said.

"You know?"

"Yes. She was in love with me."

What? I couldn't say anything. I couldn't *think* anything. Maybe my jaw actually dropped. Sage gave me space to absorb what he had said.

"You were involved with Danielle before?"

He thought for a moment before he answered. "We weren't 'involved' but, yes, I did live with her family for a few months when I first came to Paris."

"Why didn't you say anything about that earlier? Why keep it a big secret?"

"It wasn't a secret. I didn't recognize her."

"How could you not recognize her?"

"She looks completely different now – she was an awkward teenager back then. I don't see how anyone, after eight years, could have realized she was the same person. This time she was introduced to me simply as Danielle, a student teaching you French. Danielle is a fairly common name in France and nobody told me her last name."

"When did you make the connection?"

"The night after the club was trashed and all those people showed up in solidarity. We were sitting together on the floor and I told her about the first time I came to Paris and how I got to know this delightful, precocious girl in the house where I was staying. 'She didn't have your beauty,' I said to her, 'but she had your spirit. Her name was Danielle too.'"

"What did she say?"

"She started to cry. She said, 'I am that girl.'"

"When I saw you two together outside the club that night she wasn't crying. She was laughing."

"She cried and then later she started laughing about it. I think she was a little giddy."

I recalled what she said to me that night. "This has been a wonderful night. One of the most wonderful nights of my life." And the next day at dinner when I said that my summer in Paris had changed my life, she had said, "It has changed mine as well."

"Did she recognize you from the beginning?"

He nodded.

"And you're together again – 'involved' this time."

"Yes."

A couple minutes went by.

"I'm sorry," he said.

I raised my hand. "It's okay. It happens."

"She wants to talk with you."

I nodded.

"Are we still friends?"

"Sure. Of course."

He got up and started to walk out of the kitchen. When he got to the door I said, "Sage?"

He turned. "Yeah?"

I forgot what I was going to say. "Nothing." God, I was tired. I went upstairs, collapsed into bed, and fell into the deepest sleep of my life.

And then I woke up.

I had my talk with Danielle and she told me how much she cared for me. And I said and she said and I said and she said. That conversation. It's sad the way these episodes get played out in cheesy dialogue.

I had wanted to be Humphrey Bogart and lucky me, I got what I wanted – the café, the dinner jacket, the reputation, the broken heart. The whole nine yards. I was so into the bitter irony of it that I sat down and wrote a sarcastic letter to Danielle. I said I was giving her up for good, that Sage needed her at his side. I put in the exact words that Bogart said to Ingrid Bergman before she got on the plane to America in *Casablanca*. "I've got a job to do and where I'm going you can't follow, what I've got to do you can't be a part of. Danielle, I'm no good at being noble, but it doesn't take much to see that the problems of two little people don't amount to a hill of beans in this crazy world. Someday you'll understand that.

"Now, now. Here's looking at you, kid."

I was a little less bitter after I wrote it so I tore it up. Why make a total fool of myself?

CHAPTER 15

On my last night in Paris M. Duval, Sage, Danielle, Sal and I were sitting at that table in the private room in *Champ des Fraises* where we'd had supper on our first night there. We'd had a great meal and I had had a glass of wine. At 10:00 Aunt Polly Esther had left for bed but the rest of us had stayed on. Danielle and Sage did most of the talking. They went on and on about all that remained to be done with Casual Wear by Sagittarius, all that they would be doing together now that Sage would be staying in Paris. Finally they got ready to go. Sage said he would see Danielle home.

She smiled at me. She was so happy she couldn't hide it.

"Do you remember a conversation we had about stories of Paris during your first weeks here?" she asked. "About *Casablanca* and tough guys?"

I pretended to make an effort to recall. "I think so."

"I was hard on American men. Maybe you should forget."

"You had a point."

She shook her head. "No. I was generalizing. It is bad to generalize about people. But I was right about stories. The great stories are about love and politics."

I didn't see where she was taking it.

"Now you are one of the stories of Paris."

"Will they bury me in Montparnase?"

She laughed. "Maybe. Maybe you will become French. I think you are a little bit French already." She stood up and I rose to shake her hand but she bent close and kissed both my cheeks. That's how the French say good-bye.

They left and I sat back down.

"Well, Sal," I said, "That leaves just you and me."

"You and me?"

"School starts in a week."

"I'm not going with you, Rick."

"What do you mean?"

"I'm going to school here in Paris."

"You're joking. Here?"

"I'm not joking. Jean-Michel and his parents arranged it. I called my folks and they said it was okay. Actually they're kind of excited. They see it as a great opportunity."

"But Sal, you haven't told me about any of this. Not one word. And now, the day before we're to leave, you suddenly spring this on me? It's crazy."

"We haven't had much chance to talk these past weeks. You've been busy with your things, I've been busy with mine."

"Well, yeah, but something like this – I can't believe you're doing this at the last minute. Really, Sal –"

"It's not something I'm doing at the last minute. And my name is not Sal, it's Sally. Two syllables. Sally."

"But Sally," I said, "If you stay here and Sage and Aunt Polly Esther stay here, there'll be just me back in Chicago. Me and my crazy parents. I'll go nuts."

"You are such a selfish person, do you know that? All you can think about is yourself. The fact that this is a terrific opportunity for me doesn't mean a thing to you."

"It does but –" I almost said, but I'm not sure you're ready to live in Paris on your own. Sage and Aunt Polly Esther will be spending all their time on their fashion project. M. Duval has his restaurant to run. Who will look after you? Jean-Michel?

"I'll be all by myself," I said.

"Frankly, Rick, I don't really care." She got up and walked out.

A waiter came and M. Duval waved him away.

"This is the worst day of my life, " I said. Then I thought of the night M. Duval had his heart attack. "The second worst day. Two weeks ago I was the most popular guy in Paris. Now I'm Mr. Untouchable."

"I think you're being too hard on yourself." M. Duval was making parental noises. Just what I needed to send me into clinical depression.

"Humphrey Bogart. What a joke. I should have given myself Peter Lorre's part, the guy who gets killed right away. Or Sidney Greenstreet's parrot."

"This is self-pity."

"That's right, because no one else is going to pity me. Danielle said American men can't express their feelings. Well maybe that's because some of these American men have been kicked in the gut so hard they've had to take on a tough guy attitude."

"I stick my neck out for nobody."

"M. Duval," I said, "You make great desserts but your Bogart sucks.'

"Look who's talking."

We both laughed.

"Danielle didn't kick you in the gut," M. Duval said. "She has much affection for you, she has told me so many times. You fell for her because she is older and sophisticated."

"I think people in love are pretty insensitive. They're so into their own feelings it never occurs to them that other people might be having different feelings."

"That's true."

"Like tonight. Say I got a telegram telling me my folks had been killed in a car crash. Danielle would have said, 'Gee, Rick, I'm so sorry. Sage, you've just got to taste this strawberry mousse. Here, take some of mine. It's delicious."

"I don't think she would do that. Not if both parents died."

"You saw them. They might have tried just a little, made some small effort not to fall all over each other. They could have waited a few days till I left before letting it all hang out."

"They weren't so demonstrative."

"Are you kidding? It's a good thing we were in this private room."

"Sally was very quiet throughout the meal," he said, changing the subject.

"What's gotten into her? That was a rotten thing to do, springing that on me at the last minute. I'll be staying here in Paris. Bye-bye."

"I think she was angry."

"Yeah, but why?"

"Perhaps she has been disappointed also."

"What has she got to be disappointed about? She's in a funk because Warner Brothers Records hasn't signed her to a five-year contract?"

M. Duval shook his head. "You know, Rick, I don't think you see Sally. You see only this image you have of her, this Sal, your sister."

"She isn't my sister."

"No, she isn't."

"And anyway, what's so different – Sal, Sally? Different hair, different glasses. She's still Sal."

We didn't say anything for a while.

"That night when those guys sang the *Marseillaise,* she was awesome," I conceded.

"So I have heard."

But was that Sal more real than the day-to-day Sal I knew in Chicago?

"People change," M. Duval said, as if he were reading my mind. It wouldn't have surprised me if he had been. "Sally is changing. In a year or two she will be *formidable.*" He used the French word.

"Formidable?"

"A different meaning in French. What was that word you used?... Awesome. Yes. She will be an awesome beauty."

Sal, *formidable*? I mean, she had her moments at the mic, but come on. M. Duval was letting his French imagination get the better of him. She didn't need to be awesome. I just wanted her to be my friend.

"She said she didn't care if she saw me again."

" I don't think she said that."

"Well, making plans to stay here and not even telling me, that's not exactly what I'd call a gesture of friendship."

"Sometimes we do such things when we are angry."

"I still don't see why Sal is angry."

"She's in love with you."

"Sal? In love with *me*?"

"If you were able to see her, you would see that. You are her first love. The question is, will you be her last? And please respect her wishes. Refer to her as Sally."

Now I was totally confused. Nothing made sense, at least if I could believe what M. Duval was telling me. Sal, who in a couple of years would suddenly morph into the awesome, beautiful Sally, had a crush on me. I just couldn't wrap my head around it....But then that's what Sage said about Danielle – that no one could have connected the woman she was now with the teenager she had been. She had fallen in love with him and he had treated her like a child. M. Duval had an uncanny way of seeing impossible things in the future that turned out not to be impossible. He seemed quite confident of his views on all of this. You are her first love. The question is, will you be her last?

My head was spinning with questions, like those evil birds in the Hitchcock movie. I thought of Sage's challenge to Aunt Polly Esther when she interviewed him for the job of tutor: What question do you ask after asking all the questions in the universe. Answer: Have I missed anything? I seemed to have missed pretty much everything. That last question, Sage had said, opens up new possibilities. So where were the new possibilities? The next day I'd be heading back to the same old Chicago and my folks.

Meanwhile M. Duval sat there letting me stew in my juices. He would be staying here as well, when I needed him more than ever. I had come to depend on his wise, steady support. Whether or not he saw Sally clearly, he saw me very clearly.

"M. Duval," I said. "Would it be okay if I wrote to you when I'm back in the States?"

"I would like that very much," he said. "Or you can e-mail me. I realize that is the preferred manner of communication these days. I'm not on Facebook – yet." He smiled. "But I do have a laptop and I often use it."

He paused for a minute. "You know, Rick, I don't have a son. But during our time together this summer you have come to feel like a son to me. So, yes, I would very much like to hear from you. I might even come to visit you."

"You would come to America?"

"Certainly. Why not? The doctors tell me I must spend time away from my restaurant if I hope to survive into old age." Again that smile. "If I came to the States I could visit my old friend Tom Peppercorn."

"Could you manage the height and the thin air?" I asked.

"Oh yes, as long as I have my medications. I asked my heart specialist about it."

I suddenly realized I had Danielle's airline ticket in my coat pocket. I took it out, a crumbled e-ticket. I pushed it into the middle of the table.

"What is that?"

"The airline ticket to Chicago," I said. "Danielle didn't want it."

"I know," he said. "She came to me shortly after you gave it to her."

"What did you tell her?"

"I said that if she didn't want it, maybe I could use it."

I didn't know whether to laugh or to cry. But then I realized he had simply been seeing the future, as he tended to do.

"Please, take it." I told him. "Your friend at the travel agency can change the name."

"Thank you." He put it in his vest pocket. "I've been thinking. You and Tom and I should get together on that mountaintop of his. I've been sending him e-mails from time to time to keep him posted but you can't really tell a story in an e-mail. Not properly. And I think you owe him another peanut butter sandwich."

"Does Mr. Peppercorn know French?"

"He did once but he says it's gotten rusty. My e-mails to him have been in English. My English has gotten much better over the summer, I think. Have you noticed?"

Had I noticed? Good question. I needed to start paying better attention to people. "M. Duval," I began.

He reached over and put his hand on mine. "Please. Call me Louis."

At that moment I knew I loved the guy. Flat-out loved him. I wanted to tell him but there were so many emotions pushing inside me by that point I was afraid if I said the word love I'd start to cry. So I did the tough guy thing.

"Louis," I said, "I think this is the beginning of a beautiful friendship."

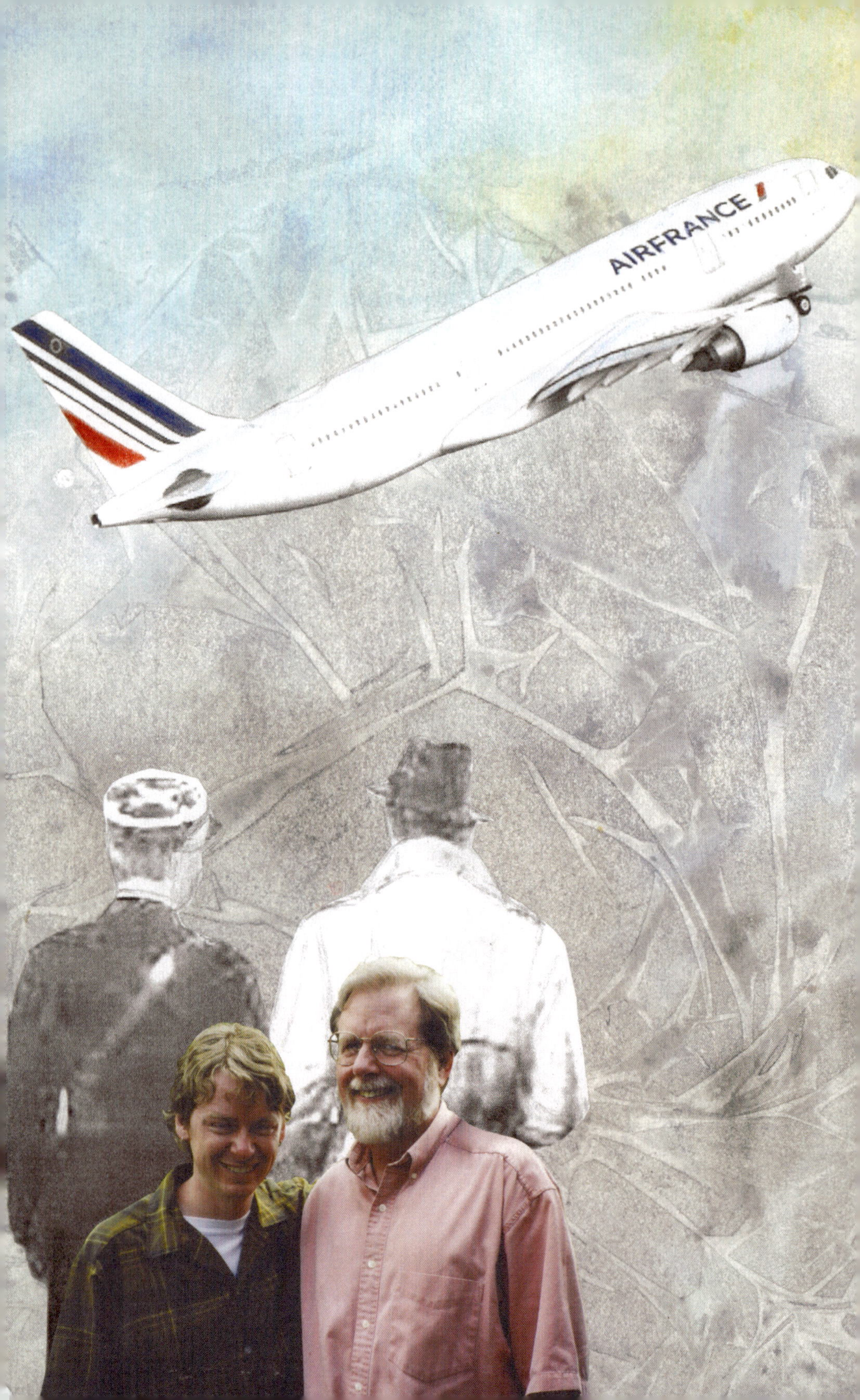
AIRFRANCE

Eric Nelson is a retired professor of literature and film studies who taught at St Olaf College in Northfield, Minnesota. He began a draft of "Rick's Paris Adventure" during a sabbatical stay in France and was assisted in its revision by his son Benno and his granddaughter Else. When his wife Riki signed on as illustrator the novel became a family project.

Riki Kölbl Nelson is a visual artist with solo and group exhibits here and abroad. She has given private lessons and art work shops to students ranging in age from six to ninety five. She's been married to Eric Nelson for over fifty years. Their collaboration on this book turned into a family adventure when their son Benno and granddaughter Else joined them with their own significant contributions.